SPECIAL MESSAGE TO READERS

THE ULVERSCROFT FOUNDATION
(registered UK charity number 264873)

was established in 1972 to provide funds for research, diagnosis and treatment of eye diseases. Examples of major projects funded by the Ulverscroft Foundation are:-

- The Children's Eye Unit at Moorfields Eye Hospital, London
- The Ulverscroft Children's Eye Unit at Great Ormond Street Hospital for Sick Children
- Funding research into eye diseases and treatment at the Department of Ophthalmology, University of Leicester
- The Ulverscroft Vision Research Group, Institute of Child Health
- Twin operating theatres at the Western Ophthalmic Hospital, London
- The Chair of Ophthalmology at the Royal Australian College of Ophthalmologists

You can help further the work of the Foundation by making a donation or leaving a legacy. Every contribution is gratefully received. If you would like to help support the Foundation or require further information, please contact:

THE ULVERSCROFT FOUNDATION
The Green, Bradgate Road, Anstey
Leicester LE7 7FU, England
Tel: (0116) 236 4325
website: www.foundation.ulverscroft.com

MURDER GETS AROUND

Murder and mayhem begin innocently enough at the Rankins' cocktail party, where Gerry Barnes and his fiery red-haired girlfriend Paula Grant while away a few carefree hours. There, Gerry meets René DeFoe, who wishes to engage his services as a private investigator, for undisclosed reasons — an assignment Gerry reluctantly accepts. But the next morning, when Gerry enters his office to keep his appointment, he finds René murdered on the premises. He puts his own life at risk as he investigates why a corpse was made of his client . . .

Books by Robert Sidney Bowen
in the Linford Mystery Library:

MAKE MINE MURDER

ROBERT SIDNEY BOWEN

MURDER GETS AROUND

Complete and Unabridged

LINFORD
Leicester

First published in Great Britain

First Linford Edition
published 2019

A catalogue record for this book is available
from the British Library.

ISBN 978–1–4448–4231–9

Published by
F. A. Thorpe (Publishing)
Anstey, Leicestershire
Set by Words & Graphics Ltd.
Anstey, Leicestershire
Printed and bound in Great Britain by
T. J. International Ltd., Padstow, Cornwall

This book is printed on acid-free paper

1

'Oh, come on, Gerry,' Paula pleaded. 'You look silly behind that desk. Besides, I promised.'

'No dice, sweet,' I said, and didn't move. 'Sam and Dot Rankin are swell people, but the riffraff you meet at their cocktail brawls give me pains all over.'

She took a slow deep breath and let the first of the danger flags unfurl in her eyes. 'Nuts!' she said. 'You've met some nice people at their parties, and you know it!'

I shook my head. 'You've got me mixed with some other guy,' I said. 'I'm your boyfriend who works for a living. Remember? But which one of the two thousand guys who almost assassinated Hitler are they entertaining this time?'

Paula Grant blew a raspberry off her luscious lips and made a face. 'Look who says he *works*!' she snorted. 'I suppose you're going to tell me you've got a case?'

I pulled open the lower left drawer and

rested my feet on it. Glancing down between my knees, I noticed the Scotch bottle with four inches left in it. I leaned over and hoisted it up.

'Speaking of a drink,' I said, 'get a couple of those glasses from that table there, will you?'

Paula didn't move. She simply sat perched on the corner of my desk and unfurled a couple of hurricane warnings. I dropped the Scotch bottle back into the drawer.

'Okay,' I sighed. 'You run along and have all kinds of fun. You can tell me all about it at dinner tonight. The Stork, about nine, huh?'

She leaned forward a little, and let one eyebrow go up the way Wallace Reid used to do it in the old silent flicker days.

'Your hearing is getting lousy, Grandpa,' she said, tight-lipped. 'I said I promised, and this gal doesn't break a promise. Which, in passing, is more than can be said of a certain dime-a-dozen private detective by the name of Gerry Barnes!'

'That's a lie!' I said in mock sternness. 'If you wore pants I'd challenge you, begad!'

'I do,' she flipped right back. 'So go ahead and challenge!'

I let that ride after a reproving look. 'You shouldn't promise things until you've consulted me,' I said. 'But honestly, beautiful, my stomach just isn't up to meeting any of Sam and Dot's European pals today. Also, I have some thinking I want to do.'

'About what?' she demanded suspiciously. Then, more on the earnest side, 'You really are on a case, Gerry?'

I was tempted to nod and look very secretive. But I love the redhead like crazy, and even conventional heels like me draw the line somewhere.

'No,' I said. 'But maybe with a little heavy thinking, I can come up with one. That is, unless you happen to know of somebody who's been robbed, rubbed out, or raped of late?'

She ignored the low humor and slid off the desk. She put a hand up to the little screwy number that in my book had no business on her queenly head, and then lowered the hand and jabbed a stiff forefinger at me.

'On your feet, mister!' she said. 'Paula has horsed around long enough. You're going to the Rankins' cocktail party. Which way is up to you.'

'But I tell you, precious — ' I began.

'I know, I heard,' she cut me off. 'Look, Gerry, I really want to go, but not alone. How's this for a compromise? An hour there, and then we'll slip away and go have fun somewhere else. Sam and Dot are so swell. They'd really feel hurt.'

Perhaps right then and there I could have established a precedent for all mankind and won an argument with a woman. But I didn't feel quite in the mood. Also, I was very fond of Sam and Dot Rankin myself. So I got up and reached for my hat.

'A deal,' I said. Then, serious-faced, 'But I'm warning you in advance.'

'Goody, goody!' she chirped. 'You mean afterward, when we go to have fun?'

'Stop it; you're a big girl now!' I snapped. 'No. I mean at the brawl. So help me, let one of those perfumed parasites make one single crack about how we do everything wrong in this country, and I'll

4

clean out the joint!'

Paula grinned, and let her lovely eyes get big and round. 'Really, darling?' she cooed. 'Oh, I do so hope somebody does. I've never seen you do any of the things you learned when you were with the Office of Strategic Services.'

'Ninety percent of that was for men only,' I grunted. 'Let's go.'

We took a cab over to where the Rankins live on West End Avenue. From the outside, it looked just like any one of lots of places. But inside, it was definitely out of this world. And that statement is strictly correct. Both Sam and Dot were born with a whole solid gold dinner service in their mouths, and a hundred times that amount in money in the bank. Beginning with their marriage right after the First Practice World War, they started going places and doing things. Not a corner of the globe did they miss, and from each one of those corners they brought back two or three things, and stuck them in their West End Avenue home. A couple of hours in there and you didn't need any Cook's Tour. You had already made one.

Their parlor, living room, or reception room, or whatever you want to call it, was just big enough for the Seventh Regiment to play musical chairs in. And when their butler let us in and took our wraps, it sounded like the Seventh Regiment was there and doing just that. All kinds of noises I had heard during the war, but this noise was the noise of them all. I stopped cold and was on the point of bellowing for the butler to come back with my hat and topcoat, but Paula had one arm linked with mine sort of half Nelson style and was moving me forward. And a few seconds later Sam and Dot Rankin popped out of a mass of milling, laughing, screaming humans and sailed down toward us.

'Thank God!' Sam Rankin gulped, and took Paula in his arms. Then, to me, 'Did you bring the Marines with you, I hope?'

'Sounds like you could do with some, Sam.' I grinned and shook his hand. 'Why not let them fight it out, and the four of us will go somewhere?'

'The four of us will not!' Dot Rankin

said sharply. 'At least not yet. I've some wonderful people I want you both to meet. Members of the underground movements in Europe during the war. Terribly fascinating, really. Sam and I first met them in the old days in Paris.'

I glanced at Sam. He didn't say anything. He just looked the words at me instead. Which were: 'What the hell, I love the gal dearly, and I'd put up with anything for her sake.'

The look came and went, and then he spoke aloud.

'Sure, come on and meet some of them. And by the way, you two, should it be Mr. and Mrs. to them?'

'My heart bleeds.' I played it with him. 'She won't have me, that's all.'

'The hell I won't!' Paula snapped. 'Get him stinking, will you, Sam? And both of you hang around as witnesses?'

'We certainly will, Paula dearest!' Dot Rankin said as the four of us started to buck our way upstream. 'And shame on you, Gerry Barnes, too! Just how long do you think you can keep this lovely woman waiting?'

I didn't get the chance to answer that, even if I'd wanted to. We were in the rapids by then, and hardly making any progress at all. Men and women, and for all I know a few of the neuter gender, swirled in on us from all sides. Sam and Dot introduced them in bunches, like grapes. I didn't catch a single name, and I didn't try. I simply nodded, smiled, mumbled inane nothings, and let myself be swept along with the tide.

But finally we came up against somebody who was really worthwhile meeting. He was a member of the Rankins' hired help crew, and he was holding a tray full of drinks in his hands. We relieved him of four instantly. And then we relieved him of four more. And then, as though they had decided to be civilized enough to allow us a short breathing spell, the mob came charging in again. When it hit, Paula's arm was linked through mine, but when it broke and spread and scattered, Paula wasn't there anymore. Somebody else had her arm linked through mine.

I looked down and took time out for a

quick blink. She was a little five-foot-one, ninety-eight pound vision in spun gold hair, china-doll-blue eyes, a cute little nose, and a pair of ruby lips that went with a cute little nose. And the smile she let those lips slide into was the best part of all.

'All this is very nice, no?'

The voice was right, too. Soft, light, and just the faintest touch of accent. I don't know why, but I guessed Vienna.

'Very nice.' I grinned. 'Now.'

She pressed my arm a little, and gave me smile Number Two. More intimate than smile Number One.

'You are Gerry, no?' she said. 'I heard that beautiful lady call you that. She is your wife, yes?'

'No,' I said. And as one of the lads with drinks edged by, I asked, 'Would you like a drink?'

'That is also nice,' she said, and let those baby-doll eyelashes flutter down.

I didn't know how she meant that. About Paula, or about the drink. Anyway, I handed her one, and took one for myself. Up came her lashes, and her eyes, as she put the cocktail to her lips. I sipped mine and began to feel considerably better. Maybe this brawl had its good points after all. And if you had seen the little number she was wearing, and how it fitted her, you would know exactly what I mean!

2

'You like it, Gerry?'

The question made me duck back and touch first. For a couple of seconds the Barnes was not being the gentleman he's cracked up to be. Maybe I even reddened a little. I don't know.

'Did you know Sam and Dot before the war?' I asked quickly.

Her eyes went a little blank, and her brows puckered.

'Sam and Dot?'

'Your hosts,' I explained. 'Mr. and Mrs. Rankin. Did you . . . ?'

'Only this day I meet them,' she stepped into my words. 'But they are so very nice. So sweet. So . . . what you call . . . ?'

'Salt of the earth,' I helped her out. Then to be gallant, 'But when Sam and Dot were racing all over Europe you must have been in . . . ' I caught myself in time. 'In kindergarten,' I said, and grinned.

Smile Three was something you'd just never believe possible. Like roses and honey. All for you!

'You are sweet, also, Gerry. I think I like you very much.'

'Mutual, I'm sure,' I assured her, and drained my drink.

And it was when I tilted my head back down that I saw her. Paula. She was sitting in a chair over by some potted palms that the Rankins had brought back from Lasha. Or maybe it was Paramaribo. Anyway, she was sitting in the chair, and sitting on one arm of it was a lad right out of your favorite heartthrob gallery. Tall, dark, flashing black eyes, trick mustache, and a he-man tan right from Cannes. Very definitely the third-act-curtain type. And if the lug moved over two more inches, he would be right in Paula's lap. And from where I stood, it sort of looked like maybe she was hoping the guy would move the couple of inches. Her face was turned up toward him, and her smile certainly wasn't the kind you'd give your landlord. Of course I wasn't jealous. That's silly stuff. I was simply annoyed at such manners in public.

'Do not look so, Gerry.'

Goldilocks' voice brought my feet back on the floor.

'Huh?' I echoed, giving her a quick down glance.

'She is so beautiful, yes. She smiled at me. Then, shaking those golden tresses, 'But René loves only himself most. Also, he is the . . . what you call . . . guest of honor.'

'Who is, and what?' I tried to cover myself.

'I have eyes, and they saw yours,' she said, still holding the smile at the Number One level. 'It is nothing with René, I assure you. And who would not speak with so beautiful a lady?'

I took another look and felt better. Pretty Boy had moved one of those two inches, but Paula had countered with an inch move of her own . . . away. I looked down at Goldilocks and grinned.

'Were my eyes that green?' I kidded. 'But René who? And what makes him the guest of honor?'

The quick look she gave me sort of

hinted that I certainly didn't get around much. I think she even looked a little disappointed.

'Then you were not of the underground?' she wanted to know.

'One of the few outfits I missed,' I told her. Then, because her eyes held a funny look, I added, 'Was that bad?'

'There was much bad in the underground,' she said slowly. 'But there was much good, too. René DeFoe was one of the leaders. But he was one of the few.'

She suddenly stopped, and let me make of that what I might. Was the handsome René one of the few leaders, and was he good or bad. At least, apparently, he looked good to Paula. For no reason at all I started to make that crack out loud. But that's all I did. I just started. Just like that, Goldilocks suddenly wasn't there anymore. She was ten feet away plowing through the crowd. Instinctively I looked ahead of her, but it could have been any one of twenty gals and guys she was going after, but fast.

Barnes, the dandy! Find 'em and lose 'em! That's him!

I scragged another cocktail from a passing tray with a waiter under it, and began a so-called nonchalant amble over toward the potted palms, and the couple snuggled under them. So snuggled that I made it to within five feet before Paula turned her head and looked at me.

'Hello, darling,' she said. 'Somebody take your dolls away? Doll, I mean? I want you to meet a most fascinating person, Gerry. René DeFoe. René, this is Gerry Barnes.'

Pretty Boy slid off the arm of the chair, showed me the nicest teeth you ever saw, and shook hands. The handshake surprised me. Like putting your hand under the tread of a Sherman tank in motion. But I just smiled instead of yelling, and he let go first.

'I am delighted, *Monsieur Barnes*,' he said, and it was an okay smile, too. '*Mademoiselle* has been telling me so many the interesting things. She says you investigate the affairs private, no?'

I shot Paula's baby innocent face a quick look, and wondered just what kind of a crack about me she had made to this iron-handed Lochinvar. But I learned nothing, so I grinned at him.

'Paula kids everybody, DeFoe,' I said. 'She meant private investigator. A cop with a civilian license. A private detective.'

He brightened, and looked very understanding. And then suddenly I thought the guy was going through the manual of arms. But I was wrong. He was simply bowing, and being very gallant to Dot Rankin, who came sweeping up. Dot gushed out something about there being somebody that Paula just had to meet, and took her in tow and was gone, leaving DeFoe and me flanking both sides of an empty chair. We looked at each other and grinned and gestured. And probably neither of us knew what the other meant by his gesture.

'You are perhaps a busy man, *monsieur*?' DeFoe finally broke the ice, and made another little gesture I didn't get. 'So many murders, so many robberies in your country?'

I hadn't liked the guy in the beginning, and I liked him less for that remark.

16

'Lots less than in some other countries,' I said, and gave him a meaningful stare.

If he got it I certainly couldn't tell as much from the expression on his face. He looked me over in frowning silence for a long moment. Somehow I kind of felt like a necktie he couldn't make up his mind on.

'But you are not too busy, perhaps?' he suddenly asked.

The business instinct in me, if I have such an instinct, was instantly on the alert. 'That depends,' I told him. Then bluntly, 'Just what are you trying to say, DeFoe?'

He didn't like that, and I didn't care whether he liked it or not. I glanced around to see if there was a nearby tray of drinks with a pair of moving legs under it. But there wasn't. When I glanced back at DeFoe, he was over his little mad, and smiling again.

'There is a little matter, *monsieur*,' he said. 'Perhaps only a matter of advice. It would be all right if I visited your office tomorrow morning? *Mademoiselle* was kind enough to give me the address.'

That he had obviously been pumping Paula about me made me sore, though I don't know why. So for a second I was tempted to tell him I was leaving that night for China. Instead, though, I stopped being silly. I was in the private eye business, wasn't I? And who says no to a customer who needs his services, and is willing to pay for them?

'Ten o'clock would be all right,' I said. And then for the sake of ethics, plus letting him know right where I stood, I added, 'But I don't accept everything that comes my way.'

He smiled at me, but it was a sad smile. Or maybe it was a little more on the envious side.

'You are most fortunate,' he said. 'With all your money, you do not have to accept *anything*.'

Damn Paula! Had she passed on to this good-looking cluck my whole family history? I was so burned at the thought that it jolted me plenty when I suddenly realized that DeFoe was staring at me with stark murder in his eyes. Only a second later, I realized that he wasn't staring at me. It was somebody behind me. I turned, but as far as I could see, the object of his glittering eyes was some more of the Rankins' imported potted palms. Not a bit of human flesh was in sight. I turned around to DeFoe and got another jolt. He was walking rapidly away just the way Goldilocks had done. Feeling very foolish, I wondered if maybe I hadn't better go out and buy some of that certain kind of soap. And also see my dentist more than twice a year.

I was still wondering a moment later when Sam Rankin suddenly appeared at my side. He had a drink in each hand. He handed me one with a weak smile.

'Have one, pal,' he grunted. 'Helps you enjoy the animal act more. My God!'

I took it, and downed it, and felt almost human again.

'Greater love hath no man for his wife, Sam,' I said solemnly. 'Or do you like things that come out of the woodwork, too?'

'God forbid!' he groaned. 'I begged Dot to skip this crowd, but I lost. I think now, though, she wishes I'd won. But she'd never admit it. I mean, she's realizing that war makes awful louses and heels out of people who were once very nice. I . . . Goddammit, what *now?*'

The last was because the constant undertone of boiler-factory sounds had suddenly become blotted out by a roaring and a bellowing and a shrilling over on the other side of the room. Sam weighed over two-ten, but he left me standing at the post. I picked up ground, though, and I was only a step behind when he went through the fringe of the group.

In the center of the group were two men. One was Pretty Boy René DeFoe, and his face was so twisted with rage it looked like it was going to fly off from between his ears. The other lad was about three-fifths DeFoe's build. A little runt that would meet up with danger in any stiff wind. And he, too, was very much riled up about something.

They were standing about six feet from each other, and screaming their lungs raw. Part of it was in French, but most of it was in a chatter that I'd never heard before in my travels. Screaming, yelling, and waving their arms like crazy. And the gathered group? They just stood there forming a circle, doing nothing but waiting for something to happen.

'Here, here, Gentlemen, please!' Sam Rankin said, and stepped between them.

If either heard, I don't know. At that exact moment, right in the echo of Sam's pleading words, the little runt shrilled something. That touched off DeFoe. His face went red, and then distorted purple. He smacked Sam Rankin's restraining hand to one side, and left the floor in a dive for the little guy. Those iron strong hands were extended out in front of him, and I suddenly envisioned the horrible picture of those hands curling around the little fellow's neck.

Well, maybe I was thinking of the little guy, or maybe just of Dot and Sam, or maybe I simply didn't care much for DeFoe. At any rate, my feet left the floor, and I made contact with DeFoe halfway to his goal in the prettiest shoulder and hip block you ever saw. It bounced him down hard, but I guess he'd had lots of experience in getting bounced down hard. He came right back up fast and tried again. He shouldn't have done that. I mean, I didn't like the guy, but I didn't want to hurt him either. But he came so fast I just had to!

It was a little elbow, knee, and head-butt trick they'd taught us in the OSS, and which I had used a few times to good advantage in both China and Burma. Anyway, it worked for me again. DeFoe went down the second time, and this time he stayed down. He was as cold as an iced herring. And I knew he would be, so I didn't give him a second glance. Training made me spin around fast. I mean, maybe DeFoe had a pal or two who suddenly didn't like me even a little bit.

No need for the spin around, however. The gathering stood right where it was, gaping and gasping. And a big lad with a back-of-a-hack face was holding hard to the little guy, and talking fast and furious in his ear. The little runt seemed not to hear. He was too busy trying to squirm away. And if there is such a thing as seeing a guy froth at the mouth, we were all seeing it then. But suddenly, he cut it all off short and went completely relaxed. His little eyes hunted out Sam Rankin, and damned if the little fellow didn't smile like a sulky, spoiled child.

'A thousand pardons, *monsieur*,' he said in a squeaky voice. 'I am desolate that such a thing should happen. A thousand pardons, *monsieur*. And to you, *madame*, a thousand pardons, also.'

He got out the last as he turned to Dot Rankin, and he almost lost balance and fell on his face, he bowed so low. And then as both Sam and Dot mumbled something, the little guy executed a snappy about-face, walked through the gathering that gave way for him, and right on out the front door, leaving his hat and coat behind. That is to say, if he had brought either.

Half an hour later, Paula and I took our leave. The near fight had brought a quick end to the party. A couple of the guests had carted DeFoe away, and the rest of them had gone hunting for their wraps. All in all, a million or so words had flown back and forth. But mostly they were apologies. I got in enough words to date Sam and Dot to meet us later at the Stork where we'd try to drink this one into forgotten memories. Then I collected Paula, and left. In the taxi she spoke her first words. At least they were the first I'd heard her speak since the shouting and the uproar.

'Poor Dot and Sam,' she said. Then, giving me a look out the corner of her eye, 'And what were you hoping to do? Break his neck just because he had been nice to me?'

I was thinking of something else, so I answered more or less automatically. 'Yeah. But I guess I'm out of practice.'

Paula sniffed and went very frigid. For once, her little act didn't have an audience. I was thinking some more. Thinking that it was certainly very poor business to slug a client *before* he'd given you the usual retainer!

3

At seven o'clock the next morning, the alarm clock reached way down into my sleep and pulled handfuls of red hot coals up out through the top of my head. I opened my eyes and then closed them quickly before my eyeballs could pop and go rolling across the floor of my bedroom. For perhaps three or four years, I lay there under the sheets waiting for blessed death to take it all away. But the fates were unkind and I went on living.

Somehow I got out of bed, and got into the bathroom to brush my teeth, and followed it with half a dozen glasses of cold water. Way, way behind all the ringing bells in my head, I remembered meeting Dot and Sam at the Stork. By mutual silent agreement, none of us said a word about the screwy cocktail party. Instead, the four of us grimly concentrated on forgetting it with fun and fizz. I said goodnight to Paula at her apartment door about five. But I couldn't remember coming to my place. I must have, though, because there I was. And with all the hangovers in the world rolled into one, and stuffed inside my one and only poor head!

Turning on the shower and stripping was more or less automatic. In back of my thoughts about last night was something else. But I couldn't pin it down in my scrambled brains and take a look. It came, though, when the needle points of icy water hit me. To be sure, to be sure! I had a business appointment with a guy at ten o'clock. But then I also remembered who the guy was, and what I had done to him. So I finished my shower, toweled myself nice and rosy, put my pajamas on again, and crawled back into bed!

At ten-fifteen I came out of it the second time and was most happy to note, and *feel*, that I was well on the way toward becoming a new man. In fact, I felt so good I even toyed with the idea of climbing on the wagon for a couple of weeks or so. My decision by the time I was dressed, and in the breakfast room on the lobby floor, was to consider the subject again at a later date.

Izzy the bootblack gave me the usual cheery greeting in the lobby of the building where my office is located, and I gave him my shoes with my feet in them one at a time, and a bright shiny two-bit piece. Then I took the elevator up to my floor. At the door of my office I stopped, stuck my key in the lock, and then stopped again. My office door was unlocked; something I make very sure it isn't every time I leave it.

In the two seconds I stood there, I decided that the charwoman had slipped for once. Then I took my key out, turned the knob and pushed open the door. I closed the door, took two steps, and really stopped short. Sitting in my desk chair and staring straight at me was Pretty Boy René DeFoe. For a second I couldn't get the words out.

'How the hell did you get in here?' they finally came with a rush.

He didn't answer. He didn't move. He didn't even blink. He just sat stiff, staring at me. And then I got a good look at that stare. I went ice cold all over, and my skin crawled in leaps and bounds. My stomach tied itself in knots, and, the breakfast I had had didn't want to stand for that sort of thing. I walked slowly forward, like I was barefoot and the rug was made of broken glass. At the front edge of my desk I stopped.

It was no crazy dream, and no poor-taste gag, either. René DeFoe was as dead as you can get on this planet.

There were some papers on my desk blotter in front of him, but I didn't give them any attention at first. I stepped around the side of the desk, and it was then I saw how he had been made dead. He had been garroted with a length of fine steel wire. The wire was sunk deep into his neck, twisted over a couple of times at the back, and the two ends drawn down taut and fastened to the bottom of the chair seat. That way he couldn't fall forward, or to either side. He could only sit there stiff, and staring out of dead eyes at whoever came through the office door. Both arms hung at his sides, and on the rug under the right hand was a fountain pen that didn't belong to me.

I let it stay right where it was, stopped looking at him, and took a look at the papers on the desk. The first one I looked at was a check on a New York bank. It was made out to me for a thousand dollars, and signed by DeFoe. The other paper was an unfinished note to me . . . on my stationery . . . that read:

Dear Mr. Barnes:
I have waited but you have not arrived. Perhaps the little affair yesterday? I assure you it is nothing. As I explained, I need your services on that most important matter. I do more so today, so I leave you this check as the beginning payment. I beg of you to telephone me at once at . . .

The letter ended there. That is, the writing of the words did, but there was a wavy line of ink down the rest of the sheet, and diagonally down my desk blotter. From there onwards was an inky scratch on my polished desk to the rear edge. Of course, it was then the wire had circled his neck and been twisted tight. No doubt he had tried to put up a struggle, but it had been no dice. Believe me, when you garrote a person, and particularly with fine steel wire, said person doesn't stand a chance, from the very first instant to the last. Not to boast, I've done it, and seen it done. But strictly under war conditions, of course.

Well, there he was in my desk chair. A very stone-dead guy who had wanted to become a client of mine, despite the 'little affair' he had considered as nothing. I looked at the check again, and was tempted to pick it up. I didn't. Instead I looked up quickly as my office door opened. What I saw was even more startling than what I'd seen when I came into the room. Ten times more startling, I guess, because the man who came inside was none other than Lieutenant Frank Bierman, of Homicide!

For a long second we locked eyes. Then Bierman lowered his, and took in all the details. He looked at me again, and smiled slowly.

'This is what I call convenient,' he said.

'The corpse and the killer in the same package.'

'Deduct fifty percent of that,' I heard myself say. 'Just the corpse. And what are you doing here?'

He broadened his dry grin a little, and made a faint gesture with one hand.

'Just a little sociable hello, Barnes,' he said. And he looked at DeFoe again. 'Who's your friend?'

I bristled at that but caught myself in time.

'A Frenchman by the name of René DeFoe,' I said. 'Was with the underground in the war. Met him at a cocktail party yesterday. He said he wanted to talk to me about something, so I made a date for ten this morning. I . . . ' I got mad again and choked on my words because of the way he glanced casually at his wrist watch. 'I got tight last night, and forgot about it!' I blurted out. 'I arrived myself only five minutes ago. Izzy and the cigar stall guy downstairs will vouch for that.'

'You gave him your office key?' Bierman asked after a long silence.

'The hell I did!' I snapped. 'The door

was unlocked when I got here. My guess is that the killer knew he was coming to see me, and got in here first somehow. When the time was right, he did his stuff.'

Bierman, the lug, looked very wise, and formed a silent O with his lips.

'I see,' he murmured. 'Then you really didn't scrag him, huh?'

I was unable to answer that for the silly rage that choked me. But Bierman didn't seem to expect an answer. He walked forward, and around in back of the desk. He looked at the way the job had been done, and nodded his head as though in silent compliment to the technique. Then he studied the check, and used up twice the amount of time necessary to read the unfinished letter. At long last he stood up and looked squarely at me.

'Of course you have no idea what he wanted to see you about?' he said more as a statement than a question.

I shook my head. 'Not even a guess,' I told him truthfully. 'He simply asked me if I was too busy, and I told him I wasn't. So we made the date.'

Bierman accepted that without further

comment. He let me alone for a few moments and made another tour of inspection all the way around the desk. He didn't touch a thing; made no move at all to go through DeFoe's pockets. I wished that I had done that myself, instead of standing looking stupid. I might have found something. But it was too late now.

'Where was this cocktail party?' Bierman suddenly asked me.

'Some people on West End Avenue.'

'What people?' he wanted to know. 'Lots of people live on West End Avenue.'

'Mr. and Mrs. Sam Rankin,' I said. 'They're always throwing parties for European refugees and such. Lots of them they knew before the war. I went with Paula Grant. It was . . . '

I shouldn't have stopped myself. Nuts to Bierman! Let him find out things for himself. But I shouldn't have stopped, so I ruined it.

'It was *what*?' he jumped at the pause.

I shadow-boxed with myself fast, and decided it would be stupid to lie. There were a lot of things about Lieutenant

Bierman I didn't care for at all, but he was a regular hatchet man when it came to his job. A very, very smart gent. Eyes and ears open twenty-four hours a day.

'It was more of a brawl than a cocktail party,' I finally said. 'I gathered that most everybody there had been in one underground or another. It was a madhouse, believe me. It ended when DeFoe, here, and somebody whose name I didn't get, got mad at each other. I helped break it up, and the party fizzled to a quick finish after that. Now you know all.'

'Maybe not,' Bierman said, and there was an edge to his voice. 'What were they fighting about?'

'It's still that way.' I shook my head. 'I don't know.'

'You didn't try to find out?' he asked with raised brows.

'No, I didn't,' I told him. Then I added, 'If you don't know French, it's a little hard to know what Frenchmen are saying.'

Bierman looked at me a moment, and then grinned. '*Vive La France*,' he said.

'You *Vive* it,' I told him. 'I can't talk to them.'

'But you took one of them for a client,' he said quickly, and nodded at the check.

'No,' I came right back. 'That check was his idea. I made the date only to listen. However, now . . . ' I checked myself once again, and of course it was the stupid thing to do.

'However, now . . . what?' Bierman tossed at me.

I started to shrug it away, but decided, what the hell? 'However, he's my client now,' I said.

'Your *client*?' Bierman echoed with a frown. 'He's dead!'

'Okay, be technical,' I said. 'His estate is my client. I'm going to find who got him, and send the estate the bill. If there is any estate.'

Bierman didn't say anything for a moment, but for once I could read his thoughts like a book. He was getting all steamed up inside. A few months before, we had both started after a murderer, and I had won. Bierman hadn't liked it at all, but there hadn't been anything he could do about it. And now it was starting all over again. Gerry Barnes vs. the recognized law. No, Bierman didn't like that a bit.

'What if there is no estate?' he asked cautiously.

I pointed at the check, and forced up a grin. 'If the law takes possession of that, then I still work,' I said. 'For free. I've always been against guys killing other guys. Especially in my office.'

He let that ride, pulled out his handkerchief and gingerly picked up my phone. I held my grin while he called Police Headquarters for the medical examiner, the fingerprint boys, and the rest of the Homicide retinue. When he hung up and looked at me, he wasn't grinning.

'Okay, Barnes,' he said. 'There's no law that says you can't. However, you're not starting here and now. I'll get in touch with you later.'

The barb stung, but I let it sting. I didn't move. I looked at him and grinned some more.

'You mean I'm getting the rush from

my own office?' I asked quietly.

He nodded and moistened his lips. 'This may be your office, Barnes,' he said, with no snarl or threat in it, 'But *I'm* telling you to get the hell out of it, now!'

I could have remained and waged, I think, a successful argument over that point. But I didn't want to. Truth to tell, I had wanted out ever since I had turned and seen Bierman standing in my office doorway. However, I didn't want him to think he was getting away with everything. So I gave him a mystifying grin, a frown, and a long thoughtful stare. Then without a word, I took a tug at my snap brim, and took my departure through the door.

In the lobby downstairs, I headed toward the phone booths with the idea of calling Paula. I wanted to let her know what had happened, and that Bierman was on the case. Also to ask her a few items I had in mind. But I decided to taxi up to her place in the East Eighties instead of talking and listening over a telephone. So I walked outside, but I didn't flag a cab that cruised by at that exact moment. Instead, I stood right where I was and watched the lad with the back of a hack face, who had held back that little frothing-at-the-mouth guy, come walking quickly across the sidewalk toward me.

4

Ugly Face stopped a couple of feet from me and started to tip his hat as they do on the Continent, even when man meets man. He checked himself, though, and smiled broadly. The smile didn't change that face any. He was still the type to scare little children, and haunt houses. And his voice was a blood relation to his face.

'Good morning, Mr. Barnes,' he said. 'We've met, but I wonder if you remember me, sir?'

I shook my head and nodded it all at the same time. Or practically, anyway. And as I didn't especially like the guy, I said: 'Your looks, yes. Your name, no.'

'Parrish, Mr. Barnes,' he told me. 'Gordon Parrish.'

As he seemed to let it go at that my eye caught the French Legion of Honor rosette in his lapel buttonhole. He noticed my glance, and I guess figured my thoughts at the same time.

'My father was American, and my mother French, sir,' he said. 'They met during the first war. My father died before the Armistice, so I've lived most of my life in France.'

I nodded and waited. If the guy wanted to tell me his life history, that was perfectly all right. Sometimes life histories are very interesting. Such as this time, for example. He waited, too, but I won.

'I wonder, Mr. Barnes, if I might have a word or two with you?' he suddenly asked.

'Certainly,' I said. Then with a glance at my wrist watch, I added with a half-smile, 'But not too many. This is one of my busy days.'

For no particular reason at all, I watched his face closely as I spoke the last. But it simply reminded me of watching the back of a hack.

'Of course, of course,' he said. And then he looked up and down the sidewalk. Then back to me with a sort of apologetic smile. 'I am not too familiar with New York, Mr. Barnes,' he said.

'Perhaps you know of some nearby quiet place where I might offer you a drink?'

I did, and it was on the way to Paula's apartment. So I took him to the Biltmore cocktail lounge. Nick was on duty and he came forward at once. I told him we wanted a quiet table, and he got the idea right away. In other words, the usual chit-chat that we pass back and forth was to be skipped this time. So he piloted us to a corner table well clear of the couple of dozen other people there, took our orders and slid away. I offered Parrish a cigarette, and held my lighter for us both. The way he puffed on his made me want to assure him that it wasn't loaded. I didn't, though. I just puffed on mine and glanced casually around. He hadn't spoken a single word since asking me where there was a place to get a drink. So as far as I was concerned, he was carrying the ball.

'That was a most unfortunate affair yesterday, Mr. Barnes,' he suddenly opened up. 'Disgraceful. René and Maurice were thoughtless swine!'

'And probably drunk,' I added dryly.

'Maurice who? And what was it about? I didn't bother to find out.'

He stared at me out of eyes that were very calculating. I would have liked very much to have known what the wheels behind them were grinding out.

'You do not ask so I assume you know René's name,' he said. 'The other one, the little one, is Maurice Cardeur. An honored soldier of France, Mr. Barnes. Though few people know it because he was of the underground, as was René, also.'

'And the reason for the scrap?' I prodded.

He frowned and took time to think that one over. He was still thinking it over when Nick brought the drinks, and left. Finally he looked across the little table at me and slowly shook his head.

'That is a mystery, sir,' he said. 'I do not know, and I cannot understand, because René and Maurice were not only comrades in arms, but the closest of friends. No doubt a trifling matter, but I do not know.'

'You didn't ask him?' I primed the

pump again. 'Or make out what they were screaming about?'

He slowly shook his head again. 'I was too busy holding and trying to hush Maurice to pay attention to what they were saying,' he said. Then with an expressive gesture, 'Of course, a word here and there, but as words they meant nothing. And, Mr. Barnes . . . '

He hesitated and looked straight at me. I suddenly noticed he had the largest pupils I'd ever seen in man or woman.

'And, Mr. Barnes,' he repeated, 'I have not been able to ask Maurice the reasons for it all, because I have not been able to find him. When he walked out of there, he vanished completely.'

'Been to his hotel room, or wherever he's staying?' I asked the obvious.

'The Hotel Green on East Seventeenth Street,' he said. Then with another slow shake of his head, 'But he has not been there since yesterday noon. I went there to see him last night, and again this morning. I was assured he did not use his room last night.'

That could mean nothing. More than a

couple of times I'd skipped using my apartment for a night. And for various reasons, too! But I looked at him, mildly surprised.

'So?' I murmured, and brought Nick's bar effort down to the halfway level.

'I do not know what to say,' he said, and gazed perplexed at his drink that was yet to be touched. 'It is most bewildering, and not like Maurice at all. And that is why I am so worried.'

'Why?' I let him have it.

He shot me a sharp glance as though expecting to see me look up absently from an engrossing book.

'Because it is not at all like Maurice to act like that,' he said firmly. 'He . . . '

'Is it like him to take on somebody twice his weight?' I cut in.

He started to look annoyed but let it fade. He finally ended up with a faint nod, and the ghost of a smile.

'I have to admit yes, Mr. Barnes,' he said. 'Maurice knows no such thing as fear. I could tell you of events in the war that would amaze you. Which you would find hard to believe, true though they were. No, a bigger man, even with a gun, would never deter Maurice. The little Lion, many of us called him.'

I nodded, and murmured something about having met up with a couple like that in my little corner of the war. And then I speeded things along by saying: 'Well, I haven't seen him, if that's what you want to know.'

'No, I did not imagine so,' he told me. 'It is for another reason I wish to speak with you. Mr. Barnes, I do not like to think that Maurice's strange disappearance is a matter for the police. You see . . . '

He paused and gave a little shrug. I just waited.

'You see, in the underground we learned to distrust the police,' he went on. 'In some cases even more than the occupying Nazis. No, I do not wish to go to the police. But you, sir, are a private detective. An investigator. Perhaps you could help me. For a consideration, of course.'

I almost grinned at the way he got out the last. So fast and together it was like a string of washing on the line.

'What would you want me to do?' I grunted, and without one half of one degree of interest. 'Find Maurice Cardeur, I suppose?'

'But most, certainly!' he replied quickly. 'I will pay you five hundred dollars now, and another thousand dollars when you have found him.'

Bingo! Or was it? I couldn't quite figure which, so I didn't say anything right away. I made table rings with my glass and thought among other things of Ballantine's ale.

'That is not enough, Mr. Barnes?' he cut into my thoughts, thinking wrong. 'I have not very much money, but perhaps . . .'

He left it hanging there. Or maybe the little half-flip of his right hand was supposed to make everything clear. As the question came to my mind, I knew it was as corny as something out of a book, but I asked it just the same.

'Do you suspect foul play, Mr. Parrish?' And then catching myself up quickly, 'Rather, have you any good reason to think he may have met with foul play?'

He toyed with that for a while, seemed

to notice his drink for the first time, and did it justice. And I do mean justice.

'You weren't by chance with the underground?' he suddenly fired at me.

I shook my head. 'No, not with them,' I said. 'But in my job I met quite a few of them. Not Europe, though. The Pacific theatre. Why?'

'You would better understand what I try to say,' he replied. 'In the underground, we were banded together for France, liberation, and the final victory. However, a man had a hundred enemies, a thousand perhaps. Unfortunately even among his own countrymen. It was not like knowing exactly who was your enemy. You follow me?'

Maybe I did, and maybe I didn't. I didn't even bother to tell myself which. I simply knew that Parrish was talking all the way around the block, and I was getting a bit tired of it.

'Sure, perfectly,' was what I told him. 'And now if you don't mind, name a few of his enemies . . . here in New York.'

The quick short cut threw him off stride. He just looked at me and blinked a little.

'Would you start with René DeFoe?' I asked before he got around to speaking.

Something happened to his eyes, and darned if I could figure it. He was either as mad as a wet hen, or ready to burst into tears.

'That would seem absurd,' he finally got out. 'They were such close friends. However, you perhaps noticed René's anger yesterday? And also his hands? He could break Maurice into pieces with those hands.'

Maybe so, and maybe René had. But right at the moment, René DeFoe wasn't even breaking his own silence. I was almost tempted for the moment to tell Parrish the news, but something held me back. Let him find out with all the others when the newspapers hit the street. Besides, I was in a hurry to see Paula before she lighted out for Lord only knew where. So instead of calling for a second round, I stood up and dropped a bill on the table.

'All right, Parrish,' I said, 'you've hired me to try and find Maurice Cardeur. However, don't count on it too much.

New York is a big town.'

He looked up quickly, a little startled, and a little perplexed. Then he looked a little disappointed. Maybe he expected we would spend the day there talking around bush after bush. Anyway, he slowly got to his feet, put a hand inside his jacket, and pulled out his wallet. As he counted out five one-hundred-dollar bills, I idly noted that he carried around quite a sheaf of the green stuff. He handed me the five hundred, and then took out pencil and paper and scribbled his phone and address over on the West Side.

'You will let me know at once, Mr. Barnes?' he said, handing me the slip of paper. Then as a second thought, 'No matter what?'

I put the money and the address in my pocket, and my hat on my head. 'No matter what, as you put it,' I said, and led the way out under the clock and down the steps to Forty-Third Street.

When we had reached the sidewalk, and a cab was rolling up to take me aboard, I half turned toward Parrish, and put a little thoughtful frown on my face.

'That business yesterday,' I said. 'For my money, they both looked ready to kill. And you said Cardeur didn't know fear. Would you also say he was the type to kill an old comrade in arms?'

I put it as a casual hypothetical question, and very much to my surprise, Parrish answered it in much the same manner. He regarded me gravely and ran a forefinger along just under his protruding lower lip.

'I believe I would stake my life, no,' he finally said. 'Maurice would be a fool to do that. The biggest fool in the world. But you will let me know anything at once, yes?'

'Yes,' I assured him, and climbed into the cab.

He watched me roll away, and then spun and beat it back into the Biltmore, but fast!

5

For perhaps the third time in fifty when I'd dropped around unexpectedly, I found Paula in. And when she opened her apartment door, the morning was definitely at the high point for me. She looked wonderful, positively. Fresh as the dew on a daisy, and as blooming as the bloom on a new rose. How she can be that way after a long night is her little secret. But she always is, and I should certainly know.

As she stepped back to let me in, she cocked a brow and looked at me down her pretty nose. Or rather, it was up.

'I'm late for a luncheon date,' she said, 'but I'll look at whatever you're selling if you promise to go away quickly.'

'Not look, sweet,' I said, and headed for the love seat next to the French windows. The liquor cabinet was right beside it. 'To listen, and then talk.'

She came over and sat beside me.

Purposely to cut off my view of the liquor cabinet.

'We're in dry-dock for this once,' she said firmly. 'Okay, I'm listening, but whether I talk is something else. So?'

I pretended I was peeved about no drink, but I really wasn't. For this once, also, it was jake by me. However, I touched a fingertip to my lips, and the fingertip to the back of her hand.

'And a dry-dock kiss for you, gal,' I growled. Then, giving her a serious look, I went on, 'It's about your French admirer, René DeFoe. And hold your horses. I'm not the jealous type.'

'Nuts, you aren't!' she said without grinning. 'So what about him? He's after you for hitting him when he wasn't looking?'

I let that go. What was the point? 'No,' I said. 'I just want to know a couple of things about him, that's all. What did he tell you about himself?'

'None of your business,' she replied sweetly. 'What did that painted little chippy tell you about herself?'

'So that's it, huh?' I grunted. 'For a

moment I honestly thought it was your usual sweet, nasty hangover speaking.'

'I never have hangovers, *Mister* Barnes! And I've decided not to buy a thing you're selling. So scram!'

It wasn't her hangover. It was mine, of course. Not saying a word, I got up and stepped to the liquor cabinet, and poured myself a little straight one. It almost choked me, but I didn't let her see that it did.

'Luncheon date?' I murmured, coming back. 'With who?'

'With *whom*, darling,' she came back quickly. 'And that's also under the heading of none of your business.'

Why do I do such things? I don't know. But I do. 'René, I bet,' I said.

She gave me one of those smiles that women give you in answer to questions like that. 'Wouldn't you like to know?'

I shook my head, and I shouldn't have. I mean, not so early in the day, even though it edged toward noon. 'No,' I said. 'Because I know DeFoe isn't the sucker for the check this time.'

All the danger flags unfurled with a

rush in her eyes, but I didn't care. When I'm troubled and worried, I never care. Maybe I should do something about that someday.

'Oh, you do, do you?' she snapped out the stock phrase. 'Well, let me tell you . . .'

She stopped as I held up one hand. 'No, let me tell you, Paula,' I said, finally disgusted myself for the way I'd handled the thing. 'René DeFoe is dead. He was murdered.'

Her partly opened mouth stayed open. But nothing else in her expression changed. She looked at me silently for as long as it takes to count five. Then she spoke. Low-voiced, and almost a little fearful, it seemed to me.

'Dead, Gerry? Murdered?'

I nodded, and on impulse took one of her hands. It wasn't cold and stiff. It was soft and warm. She was jolted, but not that jolted.

'In my office,' I told her. And then I gave her a quick word sketch of it all.

She listened with a faint frown that became a real frown when I brought

Lieutenant Bierman into it.

'What do you think?' she asked when I was all through.

'Nothing yet,' I confessed. 'There hasn't been enough time in which to do much thinking.'

'I mean about Bierman,' she said. 'Did he ever drop in to say hello to you before?'

'Never,' I told her. Then with a short laugh that wasn't mirthful, or meant to be, I added, 'Matter of fact, I never expected to see the day when Bierman would drop in . . . for a friendly visit.'

'So somebody phoned him,' Paula said, jumping way ahead. 'Somebody who doesn't like you. But who? And why?'

'No, I don't think so,' I said slowly as my thoughts started off on a rat race.

'Why not?' Paula stopped the race.

'Bierman,' I grunted, and started it again.

'Dammit, come back!' Paula blazed, and dug her fingernails into the back of my hand. 'What do you mean, Bierman?'

'Nobody in his right senses would have tried to frame me for that killing,' I said.

'Even Bierman only asked me a couple of questions. No. If Bierman was tipped off, it was simply because the killer wanted it known as soon as possible that DeFoe wouldn't be around anymore.'

'But why Bierman?' Paula persisted.

'Simple,' I said, as most of my brain continued the rat race. 'After Bierman comes the police reporters. That's what he wanted. The story on the streets as soon as possible, for all the citizens to read.'

Paula didn't comment on that. She was too busy with her own thoughts for a minute or so.

'I'll buy that little Cardeur who can't be found,' she finally said. 'And maybe even that Parrish. Ugh! He certainly has the face for murder. You say he was waiting for you just outside the building?'

I shrugged. 'Maybe,' I said. 'Maybe he was waiting, and maybe he was just passing by when I came out. Also, could be he was on his way up to see me. I wouldn't know yet.'

'Well, what *do* you know?' Then, changing it quickly, 'Rather, which of those two do you pick?'

'Hold it.' I grinned at her. 'According to the book, first comes why, then who.'

'All right then, why?'

'One of the reasons I'm here,' I said, and kissed her. 'All the others being that I like it here.'

Not Paula this morning. She pushed me away, and she meant it in her eyes, too.

'Once over again lightly, please,' she said, tight-lipped. 'Just *why* should you come here for that answer?'

'Put your hat-pin away!' I growled, suddenly sore. 'What the hell do you think I am? I.. — '

'I damn well will not!' she flared back. 'You distinctly said that first you wanted to know *why* DeFoe was murdered, so you came here to . . . '

I threw up my hands, and got to my feet. At least that stopped her. For a couple of seconds.

'Well, didn't you, Gerry?'

I counted five, with a deep breath at every count, and sat down again.

'No, Paula, no,' I said as calmly as I

could. 'I didn't. I definitely didn't. I simply came here to ask you some questions about DeFoe, and — '

'And what in hell could I tell you about René DeFoe?' she broke it up again.

'Maybe nothing,' I said, pushing down harder than ever on the brakes. 'Maybe nothing at all. But I got the idea he asked quite a few things about me. And in case he didn't mention it to you, he wanted to see me about something this morning. We made a date for ten, as I told you a moment ago. I'm simply wondering if he said anything yesterday at the brawl that you might be able to now connect up with what's happened.'

The anger faded from her cheeks and out of her eyes. She looked at me, and a funny little smile hovered at the corners of her mouth. 'If you'd only marry the gal, Gerry,' she said, 'I'm sure we'd never have spats like this. They'd be so silly.'

'They're silly now,' I skipped it over. 'Well, did he say anything . . . that makes more sense, now? Talk to you about his service in the underground? Things like that?'

She took a few seconds to think that over, and then shook her gloriously red-topped head.

'No, not a thing I can remember, darling,' she told me. 'But he did ask questions about you, and seemed very interested in the answers. But I just thought he was being polite, because he'd seen us come in together.'

'He knew who I was?' I asked.

'No. But he asked, and I told him. Was that wrong?'

'At such close quarters, yes,' I grunted, remembering. 'He didn't tell you why he wanted to see me, did he?'

She shook her head and opened her mouth. But no words came off those nice lips. The sudden clanging of her phone stopped them. She got up and went over to it on a little corner table. I got up and went over to the liquor cabinet. I was lifting the jigger when Paula's voice speaking into the phone came drifting over to me.

'Yes, this is Miss Grant. Who? Oh, yes, yes. Mr. Barnes? Why . . . why, he happens to be here now. Would you like to speak to him? Just a minute, please.'

I had turned just as Paula had turned her head, and if looks could knock you kicking, I would still be bouncing. She put one hand over the mouthpiece and spat verbal ice cubes off her tongue.

'She would like so ve-e-e-ry much to speak wiz zee dear Me-e-e-ster Barnes. The nerve of her calling here!'

'Who?' I said, and stared.

'Your baby doll!' Paula shot back. '*Mademoiselle* Zaralis.'

'Cut the gag,' I said. 'I don't know anybody by that name.'

'Oh, yes you do,' she replied, bittersweet. 'Intimately! At Dot and Sam's yesterday. The little blonde cloying number that had you on the merry-go-round. She probably wants the brass ring back!'

That one, huh? So I had been wrong guessing it Vienna. It was probably Athens, or maybe Istanbul. I walked over and took the phone from Paula. Her sniff and the tilt of her nose rubbed me the wrong way.

'Hello, *Mademoiselle*,' I said into the phone. 'This is Gerry. How are you?'

It was Goldilocks right enough. Her voice rippled along the wire like agitated honey. 'Oh, Gerry, I am so glad I find you! Are you so very busy, no?'

'No, I guess not,' I told her after a moment's hesitation. 'Why?'

'There is something I would like to tell you, Gerry,' she said. 'But not now. Could you come to my apartment, at once? It is not too far. Just a little way from you, on Park Avenue. You will come at once, please, Gerry?'

All of it didn't make sense to me. But maybe it would after I'd seen her. One thing was sure: she'd known DeFoe well. Maybe more than just well. I might be able to find out some things, though just what things I wanted to find out I wasn't so sure of myself . . . yet. I asked her for the Park Avenue number, and she gave it to me. Just a block over and two up from Paula's.

'And please come right away, Gerry,' she insisted. 'I think perhaps I am a little worried about something. You will try to help me, yes?'

'Okay, I'll be there,' I told her.

Her goodbye was tinkling silver bells, and a split second before I started to lower the phone I caught Paula's look out of the corner of my eye. She was burning so you could almost see the flames and the smoke. By way of paying back for her having gone off the handle, I eased out the hand she couldn't see and broke the phone connection.

'But wait a minute!' I spoke into the dead phone. 'You'll be in bed at eleven-thirty, won't you? Huh? Okay, then. Swell! Yes, I'll be there. S'long.'

With that I hung up and walked over toward Paula, feeling the very clever comic that I wasn't. I waited for Paula to speak, and I didn't have to wait long.

'And will she, Romeo?' she asked in a funny voice.

I looked at her, wide-eyed, and blinked. 'Will she *what?*'

'Be in bed at eleven-thirty!' she gritted. 'You two-timing heel!'

I had my laugh at her expense, and then explained how that part had just been for her benefit. Punishment for her flare-up. And then the boomerang came around in back to catch me on the noggin! Paula wouldn't believe me. I was so dumbfounded that she had her apartment door open, and was handing me my hat, before I had a chance to come up for air.

'Have fun, darling,' she said icily. 'And here, think of little Paula sometime.'

She accompanied the last by dragging down my head and kissing me hard on the cheek two or three times. Then she gave me a little push, and slammed the door in my face. I stayed stunned for a couple of moments longer; then I really felt the heel that I was. I worked the doorbell button hard, and banged on the door itself. When my knuckles got good and sore, so did I. I went over and down in the private elevator. The doorman at the main entrance looked at me and grinned from ear to ear. I was just about to ask what the hell he was grinning about when I caught a flash of my face in one of the door high narrow mirrors that flanked the entrance. One cheek from eye to jaw line was a mess of lipstick smears.

I glared at the doorman, yanked out my

handkerchief, and hurried out onto the sidewalk. A cab came cruising into the curb just as I got there. I opened the door and ducked inside, and started to give the driver the Zaralis dame's address, but I didn't go through with it. I didn't because at that moment a thin-faced, funny-looking character strolled by. Not fast, and not slow. Rather, just the right pace to be abreast of the open taxicab door, so as to catch what I said. Maybe a tail put on me by Bierman, or maybe a tail put on me by somebody I didn't know. Then again, maybe I was all wet. However, I decided to play it the sure way, if possible.

'Radio City!' I barked at the cab driver, and pulled the door shut.

6

After three blocks, I was as sure as I needed to be. Thin Face had popped into another cab and was coming right along behind me. And it was obvious that he had given his driver strict instructions. Twice at a red light the other cab could have pulled up alongside, and been set to go with us from scratch on the green. But no. Each time the other cab slowed and pulled in behind a couple of other cars. When you see a New York cabby do *that*, you can bet the works he's been given his instructions.

'What number Radio City, mister?'

My cab driver's voice jerked me back from my rambling thoughts. For a moment I was tempted to tell him the set-up, and let him do his stuff to lose the cab behind. But I checked that. No sense letting Thin Face know that I knew I was being tailed. I might want it the other way around at some future date.

'Thirty Rockefeller Plaza,' I told my man.

A few moments later he pulled up, and I paid him what it said on the meter, plus. I was out and going through the doors as the other cab pulled up. So once I was through the doors I put on speed. If you've never been inside Thirty Rockefeller Plaza, or the RCA Building as it is known, let me mention that it is even better than Grand Central Station when it comes to shaking off a tail. You could even shake off your mother-in-law in that man-made labyrinth and not have to shift out of second gear.

Ten minutes later I came up out of the ground on Fifty-Ninth near Sixth, timing it just right to nail the only flag-up cab in sight, and away I went. To double check, though, I took a ride around Central Park before telling the driver to cut over toward the Zaralis woman's address.

Her apartment was on the fourteenth floor, and she answered my ring almost before I could get my finger off the button. Smile Three was all for me, and she used both hands to pull me inside, which was quite unnecessary considering.

'You are so sweet, Gerry,' she purred, and still clung to my one mitt with her two. 'You come so quick, no?'

By then we were in a sort of sunken living room that was definitely not furnished with junk picked up here and there. Quite the contrary. It was very high-priority stuff, and in good taste, too. Whoever paid the bills was in the chips. And I certainly didn't think that Goldilocks had paid the bills. Maybe it was either one, or both, of the two chaps I saw right after I'd taken a sweeping look at the layout.

Both were about the same age. I pegged it at between thirty and thirty-five. Both were about the same build, too. But it all ended there. One was a redhead; a real carrot-top, too. His face was round and ruddy, with quite a splash of freckles across the bridge of his nose. His eyes were a funny-looking washed-out blue, and in the lapel buttonhole of his jacket he wore the U.S. army discharge button.

The other man was dark, very dark. Dark hair, dark eyes, and a matching complexion. Several countries in South America, and also Spain, came to mind as I looked at him, but I couldn't be sure. But by then Goldilocks had pulled me close and was making the introductions. The lad with the flaming hair was Andy Parkus, and the other fellow was introduced to me as Henri Barone.

We all shook hands, sized each other up, and probably postponed decision. At least I know I did. Then I had a drink in my hand, and I was sitting on a couch with Goldilocks. We all took a drink, smiled around, and seemed to wait for somebody to break the ice. I elected myself.

'What outfit, Parkus?' I inquired pleasantly.

'Hundred and Tenth Tank Destroyers,' he told me.

I nodded, and lifted him up a notch in my silent appraisal. 'One of the best,' I murmured politely.

'*The* best,' he said quickly. And then he grinned at me as though waiting for me to make something out of it.

I didn't. He had just about called it. If

you look back in your newspaper files to March and April of 'Forty-Five, you can read all about the One Hundred and Tenth. They wrote a chapter in war history that'll be around for a long time. No doubt as long as people can read.

'Saw some of it in the OSS, didn't you?' he asked me presently.

'Some of it,' I admitted, and let it rest at that.

Frankly, the situation was getting under my skin. I hadn't expected Goldilocks to have company in her lap. And in the second place, we were all just sitting around twiddling our thumbs, and getting noplace. Then, suddenly, I thought I had it. No doubt Parkus and Barone had dropped in between Goldilocks' phone call to Paula's and my arrival. So I finished my drink, glanced at my wrist watch, and stood up.

'I just dropped by to say hello.' I grinned down at her. 'And I must be chasing along. So . . . '

'But no, Gerry!' she cut me off, and pulled me down again. 'You do not understand. It is Andy and Henri who wish to speak with you. They were at the affair yesterday. You did not meet them, no?'

I had not met them, or even seen them, as far as I could recall. Unsurprising, since a fairly good crowd had been crammed into Sam Rankin's place. So I took the refill she pressed into my hand and looked politely inquiringly over at Parkus. He grinned, but said nothing. I didn't like that grin. I switched my gaze to Barone, and found him really giving me the X-ray treatment. In a nice sort of way, but still the treatment nevertheless.

'You recall that stupid fight, *monsieur*?' he suddenly asked.

The lad's accent intrigued me. It was unlike any I'd ever heard. I was curiously reminded of a screwy Englishman I once met who was always trying to give the king's language the Seine Left Bank touch.

'Certainly I recall it,' I finally told him flatly. 'Why?'

He seemed to mull that over, and I thought I saw him shoot a questioning look at Goldilocks.

'The small one was named Maurice Cardeur,' he said slowly. 'He was my close friend, and so I am worried.'

'Worried?' I murmured. 'Why are you worried? Has something happened?'

Once again I thought I caught him shooting that silent eye question at Goldilocks. But I checked myself from turning to see if she gave him an answer. I looked at Barone's face, and thought of soap and a washrag.

'That is why I am so worried, *monsieur*,' he said. 'Because I do not know. Maurice left immediately, if you recall?'

My nod told him that I did.

'That was the last that I . . . or any of his friends . . . have seen of him,' Barone said. 'He did not return to his hotel. I do not know where he went. So I am worried. Maurice does not know New York so well. Perhaps . . . '

He dropped it there, and then added the shrug, the two-handed palms up gesture, and the lift of the eyebrows. I still let him see that I was only mildly interested. Which of course I wasn't.

'Maybe having made such a fool of

71

himself drove him out of town for a day or so,' I said dryly. 'Maybe he just wanted to hide his face for a while. Incidentally, what was that argument about? I didn't find out.'

'It was silly,' Goldilocks spoke up; a little too quickly, I thought. 'A silly, stupid, personal matter. René insulted Maurice for the clothes he was wearing. And Maurice cannot stand insults. Not even silly ones.'

I grunted, and felt like telling her to go back to school and come through again with an improved brand of quick thinking. Instead, though, I just went right on looking at Barone. He hadn't carried the ball far enough yet for my money.

'It was very silly,' he echoed Goldilocks' comment. 'But you would better understand if you knew Maurice as I do. As Zara and Andy do too.'

Zara for short? Or Zara Zaralis? I'd maybe find out later. I had some of my drink and liked every bit of it. Then I decided time was a-dallying.

'Have you any reason to think that something's happened to him?' I asked.

'And why would you want to see me about him, anyway?'

'I do not know what to think,' he answered cautiously. 'That is why I am worried. As for you, *monsieur*, is not finding people your business, yes?'

'The Missing Persons Bureau would do the same thing for nothing,' I said.

He didn't like that. He didn't like it at all. He scowled, and when he did it made his face almost midnight.

'No!' he said sharply. 'The police, no. You must understand, *Monsieur* Barnes. Maurice is a Frenchman. He is but visiting your great country. If he caused trouble for the police authorities, his visit might be made shorter. Maurice does not wish to return to France immediately.'

I looked at him, and took a shot in the dark.

'Not quite safe enough yet, huh?' I grunted.

'Exactly,' he said, nodding. Then right on top of it, 'But do not misunderstand that also. Not all those who wished to betray France to the Nazis have been arrested, or met with suitable justice. We of the underground who fought so long may have to go on fighting as long as we live. I mean, *monsieur*, against those countless traitors who betrayed our country at the very beginning.'

So he was French? Could be. 'I see what you mean,' I murmured. Then, to hasten things, I went on, 'And what really worries you is that maybe one of those enemies followed him over here?'

'Yes, yes, that is exactly what worries me!' he almost tromped on my last couple of words. 'So you see why I cannot go to the police? It would be in the newspapers, and we do not wish things about us to be in the newspapers.'

I wanted to ask him flat out what were the ten other real reasons he and his pals were publicity shy, but I let it go. Three or four, or maybe just a couple of the pieces of this newest cockeyed puzzle, were beginning to fit together in the old brain. So I gave him another understanding nod, and then twisted my features into the thoughtful pose.

'Do you connect up his strange disappearance with René DeFoe?' I asked. 'They certainly wanted to go at each other's throats yesterday.'

My words were greeted with very sudden silence. Parkus held his more or less perpetual grin, but it froze up a little. Barone looked at me as though he expected me to go on and say more. And from what I could catch of Goldilocks out of the corner of one eye, she looked like somebody had cracked an off-color story that wasn't even funny. I mean, she didn't know whether to laugh, or call for the butler to usher the bum out.

'DeFoe has a fool's temper,' Barone finally broke the silence. 'But he is not a fool, as he would like some to believe. No, I cannot conceive of any possible connection there. DeFoe would not dare!'

Whatever he meant by all that was passing me by. I felt like saying, though, that maybe DeFoe had dared . . . and come out second best. Instead, I said the very same words I had spoken to another lad interested in Cardeur's whereabouts a little over an hour before.

'What do you want me to do? Find Maurice Cardeur, I suppose?'

He nodded and slipped a wallet from his pocket. He zippered it open and started taking out lengths of government green. When the pile on the coffee table between us totaled a thousand bucks, he zippered the wallet closed and put it back in his pocket.

'A thousand dollars for you to find Maurice Cardeur,' he said. 'Another thousand dollars if you are able to find him within twenty-four hours.'

I glanced at the money, but I grinned at him. 'Dead or alive?' I asked.

He had taken too big a lead, and that picked him right off the bag. It really jolted him, and for several seconds he couldn't find the words.

'Dead or alive, *Monsieur* Barnes,' he finally managed. 'But it is absurd to even think of Maurice as dead.'

That just didn't jell after all the beefing about being so worried about the guy. But I skipped that, too. I picked up the money and nodded at him. Then I slipped the money into my pocket. Yes, the same pocket that held Gordon Parrish's five hundred. The little guy, Cardeur, was certainly becoming quite a gold mine for me. A total of fifteen hundred in cash so far from two guys to find him.

Dead or alive!

7

All the time, Barone watched me put the money away like it was maybe his right arm, or a leg, he had given up. Then he licked his lips, and took out a silver pencil and a little pad of paper.

'I had better give you the hotel address where he was staying,' he said. 'It is the — '

'The Hotel Green on East Seventeenth,' I cut in on him. 'I know that. How about places where he hung out when he wasn't at the hotel? And did he have any lady friends?'

I sensed Goldilocks stiffening at my side, but I was all eyes for Barone. He looked like the apple had been rotten and chock-full of big juicy worms. And then suddenly like a flash, a look came over his face that made it my turn to be startled. Maybe you could call it like that of a surprised cobra. Anyway, it wasn't nice to see.

'You know where he was staying?' he asked sharply.

Even Parkus' grin had faded, and his washed-out blue eyes were fixed on me stickum tight.

'Why, sure,' I tried to cover up fast. 'The Rankins mentioned it last night. We were talking about DeFoe and Cardeur. I went out with them later.'

Neither Barone nor Parkus believed that one, and I was sore at myself for letting the urge to see him jolted get the better of me. Ten to one he knew as well as I did that probably neither Dot nor Sam had the faintest where any of their brawl guests holed up. And now cared a damn sight less, you might be sure.

'But what about his lady friends, if any?' I went on forcing it. 'Have you tried them?'

'There are none, *monsieur*,' Barone said just the way you'd say it if you were thinking of ten other things. 'Maurice was not . . . what you call . . . a ladies' man. No, it would be senseless to *cherchez la femme*.'

'Okay, I won't,' I said solemnly. 'But

what about you? I mean, how do I get in touch with you, if and when I have something to report?'

'I shall also be searching, of course,' he said after a long pause. 'So perhaps you will inform *Mademoiselle* Zaralis of what you find out, eh? I shall also keep in touch with her. That is perfectly agreeable, Zara?'

The last was to her, and I know damn well that something unspoken went along with the look he gave her. She nodded, and pressed one knee to mine as she did it.

'But most certainly, Henri!' she exclaimed. 'I shall remain here constantly and pray that good news about Maurice will come so very quickly.'

'Thank you, Zara,' he said. Then, beaming at me, 'And a thousand thanks to you, *monsieur*. I feel much less worried already, now that you have consented to help us. We will meet again soon, is my prayer, also. Meantime, may the good fortune search with you.'

Very pretty, very neat, and very, very fast. I almost wondered if they'd rehearsed it a couple of times. Anyway, just like that, Andy and Henri had taken their departure, leaving Goldilocks and me all alone on the couch.

'Poor Maurice,' she murmured. Then, with a little of that bell-tinkling laugh, she added, 'But it is silly for Henri to worry so. Nothing bad could ever happen to Maurice. He is so . . . Oh, Gerry, dear, your drink!'

She fluttered her hands a couple of times and then reached over in front of me for my empty glass. Such perfect timing you never did see. It was a case of being a man or a mouse. And who would want to be a mouse to that little doll? Her lips were very top-rating. And all the rest was strictly par, too. That is, if you go for an atom bomb in a hostess gown. But eventually I got my new drink, and twisted around a little . . . the better to see her, and be prepared.

'What's the Zara?' I asked. 'Nickname, or what?'

'It's the what.' She grinned at me. 'My first name. You like it, Gerry?'

'So-so,' I grunted. 'I think I like

Goldilocks better. And you know something?'

She quickly reduced the four inches between us and went wild with the baby-doll-eye technique. 'Lots of the things, Gerry,' she purred. 'But perhaps that is not what you mean, no?'

'Nope, and nope again,' I said. 'I mean, you look too cute a little trick to have such tramps for friends.'

'Tramps for friends?' She blinked, and frowned at me.

'Strictly from tramps,' I said. 'Maurice, René, Andy, and Henri. And a lad named Parrish, too. You know Parrish, don't you?'

You would have thought I'd smashed a lot of wet leaves into her pretty little face. She jerked back from me and spilled a lot of her drink on the rug that had set somebody back two thousand if a dime. She didn't seem to notice. I was the object of her attention. As intensely as I had been of her affection half a shake before.

'You know Gordon Parrish?' she practically spat at me.

A hunch told me it was suddenly very thin ice, so I looked surprised, and put a lot of hurt into it, too.

'Hey, what gives?' I demanded. 'Shouldn't I? Actually, though, I don't really know him. Met him at that lovely party yesterday. He was the one who was trying to stop Cardeur from climbing all over DeFoe. Why? Something wrong with Parrish?'

She paused, then looked very sorry, and came cuddling back like a little kid. A little kid with all the answers!

'He is a swine!' she had enough left to hiss out. Then, 'I am so sorry I get mad, Gerry, sweet. It is not the fault of yours, of course. But if you really knew Gordon Parrish, you would call him a swine also. And think so. But the others, Gerry — they are not . . . not the tramps. They are my friends, my dearest friends. I think I would like you, too, to be my very dearest friend.'

Deep water, and rough, ahead. And I had only brought one set of oars! I decided we both needed a cigarette. And that way I was able to get up and go over to a little table where there was a tray of them. Why bother with the pack in my jacket pocket? We used my lighter but I remained on my feet.

'Look, Goldilocks,' I suddenly popped at her. 'Deep friendship is a wonderful, wonderful thing. But to go overboard a thousand dollars' worth sort of makes a fellow wonder. Particularly a fellow like me who did go beyond the fourth grade. What's it all about, anyway?'

She gave me those baby eyes, but switched to the graver variety when she saw I wasn't buying. 'Maurice Cardeur,' she said quietly. 'Maurice is missing. His friends cannot find him.'

I looked at my watch, then down at her. 'Missing for fifteen hours,' I said dryly. 'So what? I've been missing from my dearest friends longer than that lots of times. And nobody ever put up ten cents to find me.'

'You do not understand,' she murmured, and stopped meeting my eyes.

'You can say that again,' I grunted. Then quickly, 'Have you seen or heard from René DeFoe today?'

No dice, if I hoped for anything. She gave me her eyes again and shook her head.

'No, Gerry,' she said.

'Andy or Henri mention seeing or hearing from him?' I probed.

Did she hesitate, or was it just being one of those slick dicks out of a two-dollar book?

'No,' she said. 'We talked only of how strange for Maurice to disappear. And I told them you were the private investigator. And that perhaps you would help us. So I phone you.'

'Wrong,' I said. 'You phoned Paula Grant.'

'But of course!' she exclaimed, and her eyes went wide in surprise. 'There is no answer at your apartment, so I call Miss Grant. Perhaps she can tell me where you are. And you are there. So?'

A question hovered on the tip of my tongue, but I didn't let it drop off. Frankly, I was beginning to have a few doubts. Maybe certain guys are screwy enough to put up a thousand bucks to find a pal when he'd only been unseen for a mere fifteen hours. Anyway, I had the firm feeling that a lot of questions I had planned to ask Goldilocks wouldn't so much as get me sacrificed down to second.

'You will find Maurice, I am sure,

Gerry,' she suddenly popped off. 'Well, and quite happy, too. And so we forget Maurice for a few moments, and have another of the drinks, yes?'

Before I could give her a yes or a no, the phone rang. It was in another room. Her bedroom. She looked startled, and then poutingly annoyed. She got quickly to her feet, and then came way up on her tiptoes. Naturally I didn't want her to fall on her face, so I had to do the right thing and catch her.

'You make the drinks, darling!' she choke-whispered. 'I will tell who phones me that I am not home. Most certainly I am not home for hours and hours, yes?'

I grinned and sent her on her way toward the phone in the bedroom. Goldilocks could certainly make it a chore for a guy to earn his retaining fees!

I made two new drinks, and then drank one of them, she took so long. But I had that one remade by the time she came back. One look and I was strangely glad. The Barnes was not going to have to face the acid test, because it wasn't going to be hours and hours like she'd said.

'Gerry,' she said, as though the tears were close, 'I am so desolate.'

'Well, it becomes you, baby,' I said lightly, and waited.

She walked over to me, stopped, put one hand on my arm, and looked up at me, oh so very close to tearfully.

'You will not be mad, Gerry?' she practically lisped. 'You will not hate me, no? It is that I forget the things completely. I have the appointment for lunch. It is impossible to say that it must be for another day. You will forgive me, sweet Gerry?'

Truthfully, that was quite okay by me. The party had been heading along lines I didn't care about right at the moment. Besides, I had things to do myself. Among them, feeding the inner man. However, for future occasions, in the event there might be future occasions, I looked and let myself sound just a wee bit disappointed. Then in due time and course we parted at her apartment door, and I jumped the elevator downward.

When I reached the sidewalk my head was full of thoughts, and not all of them were pleasant ones. Still thinking, I ambled to the curb and flagged a cab that was curving inward. I opened the door and started to give him my office address, but I never finished it. The back of the cab suddenly fell down on my head, and I went sailing off into a world filled with nothing but darkness and silence!

8

'He's comin' around now.'

The words came to me from a long way off. From way over beyond a great big black cloud that was pushing against my face. Spoken words, but they didn't mean a thing to me. No sense at all. It was like coming on a lighted neon sign in front of a restaurant that was closed and boarded up tight. Meaningless, because there was nothing behind it but darkness. With me, though, it was behind, in front, all around, and inside too. Nothing made sense. That is, save for a couple of items. There were firecrackers in my brains, and my very own little world was total darkness.

I made myself open my eyes, but that didn't change anything. Still total darkness. The single word, blindness, forced its way in among the firecrackers, and terror promptly struck way down into my guts. As it really started to lash around the blessed gods on high made a couple of other items make sense. I mean, I realized that I was blindfolded, but tight. And that my hands were tied behind my back, but tight also. Item five followed instantly. I was sitting on a chair. The wooden kitchen variety. Which is to say, one leg was a fraction shorter than the other three. It teetered a little as I impulsively shifted position. And that brought more words again. From just off the end of my nose.

'Open up for papa, Barnes.'

The lip of a glass was wedged between my lips, and a very lousy brand of rye slid by and down my throat. Lousy stuff, but at least it did some of the work necessary. It brought back the power of speech. Gurgling, and gasping, but nevertheless speech.

'Where the hell am I?' I demanded.

That brought a harsh laugh from one. And a dry, mirthless chuckle from a couple of others.

'It ain't up in Mabel's room, Barnes,' said the voice that was closest. 'Want another?'

Thoughtlessly I shook my head. It almost fell off and rolled down my chest.

'What is this?' I kept at it. 'Who are you guys? And what's the idea of the rough act?'

A second voice answered that one. He seemed quite a way from me, giving me the impression that I was in a fairly large-sized room.

'Just making it easier all around,' he said. 'The answers to a few questions, that's all.'

About that time I came to realize that they hadn't bound my legs. And promptly the fathead in me toyed with the idea of popping up and kicking whoever was right in front of me where it would be hurt the most. I managed to kill the urge, though. At least postpone it for a spell. That would depend on how long it took to glue back the pieces of my broken head.

'What questions?' I asked. 'Questions about what?'

'Oh, this and that,' the voice in the distance told me. 'And we're not in any hurry, Barnes.'

'I am!' I snapped. 'I suddenly don't like it here.'

I popped up to my feet and started a beautiful goal from the field. However, the side of my foot simply grazed somebody's leg, and momentum slammed me over and down flat on my back. I was swimming in bursting colored stars as somebody hauled me up and plunked me down into the chair.

'Just a tough guy, but dumb, eh?'

The words were accompanied by a ringing smack across my left cheek. Not hard enough to knock me out. Just enough to let me stick around and watch all those busted colored stars go parading by.

'Be bright, Barnes,' I managed to hear the distant voice advising me. 'Just the answers to a couple of questions, and then you can run along.'

I didn't say anything to that. The parade of stars had passed on, and I was trying to make connections between my straining ears and what undamaged brains I had left. The voice near me had been hard, and surly tough. Like from the lips of maybe a big guy. The distant voice was reedy. From a thin-faced guy? Maybe the thin-faced guy I'd ditched in Radio City? And while I was straining for sounds, I picked up some that were quite familiar. They told me things, but considering the situation not very important things.

Boat foghorns told me I was very close to either the East or Hudson River. They told me also that it must be night, because the skies had been cloudless the last time I'd been in a position to look. And then a different kind of rumbling roar made me elect the East River as my best guess. I mean, I was sure I was close to where Long Island traffic, to and fro, was crossing one of the bridges. But which one I didn't bother to guess.

'You fake lousy, Barnes!' the tough hard voice broke into my ears and brain efforts. 'Come out of it!'

A light rap on my nose was a warning. It stung, but not enough to make me play sucker to a smash on the jaw.

'We've plenty of time, but not all the time. What did DeFoe say to you yesterday?'

'Who's DeFoe?' I came right back.

He'd warned me to be bright, so I got it. A smack that seemed to loosen every one of my teeth. They were certainly playing in a blue-chip league.

'What did DeFoe say to you yesterday, Barnes?'

I could have laughed that off, too, but I wasn't in a humorous mood. 'Nothing particular, that I remember,' I said. 'We just batted the breeze. Were you one of the six million there, too?'

'Right,' he admitted. 'And you didn't bat any breeze with that baby. He made a date at your office for this morning.'

I thought of DeFoe's angry glare that had made me turn around and see nothing but imported potted palms. It appeared now that there had been somebody. And that somebody had heard us make the date. The killer? This character who owned the reedy voice in the distance?

'Then why ask me?' I played for time.

'Nobody's asking you *that*,' he gave it to me pointedly. 'Why did he want to see you?'

'I don't know,' I said truthfully. And then as I sensed movement close, I added quickly, 'And tell this plug-ugly here that slugging me won't change that at all. I just don't know!'

'No?'

'No!'

'You're a goddam fool, Barnes! Did you know that?'

'When I flag my next taxi I won't be,' I told him. 'But how's for letting me ask a question?'

He gave that a moment of silent thought. Or maybe he looked at the others to see what they thought. Because of my little world of darkness, I couldn't tell. 'All right,' he eventually decided. 'Let's have it.'

I had about forty questions I wanted to ask, but I figured I'd only be able to get in one. I couldn't make up my mind which one I wanted to know about most.

I decided to take a long, long chance. 'Why was DeFoe scragged in my office?' I demanded.

Silence. A great big carload of it. I could hear three different kinds of heavy breathing. Like three guys who had been running like hell for a long time.

'Once again, Barnes?' the distant voice asked, and I could almost picture his lips stiff and back against his teeth . . . if he had teeth.

'Why was DeFoe scragged in my office?' I repeated. And then because I seldom let well enough alone, I added, 'I didn't ask who . . . I asked *why*? The other one, I know!'

And, of course, not having been the type to let well enough alone, I walked myself right into a terrific beating. The guy nearest me, I think it was. Or maybe the owner of the third voice I hadn't heard yet. Anyway, I got hit on the right jaw, and went spinning over to the left. I didn't go all the way because a smash on the left side of the jaw straightened me up. Then one to the mouth drove my head straight back. By then I was getting around to doing something about it.

Something, but so very, very little. I did, though, come up onto my feet, and all the rough and tumble with hands tied that I'd learned and put to use in the OSS came to my rescue. But it came just a little bit late. I got in a couple of head butts, and I kicked a couple of shins, and also other parts of the human form. I even worked a leg trip-twist that dropped somebody like a ton of bricks. And then just as the bellow of pain was starting to be music in my exploding ears the whole damn works came down with a crash, and there I was under it all. But I didn't know about that. All I knew was strictly from nothing . . . for the second time in one day!

9

It was all so peaceful and nice that I felt like somebody had played me the dirtiest trick in the world when I opened my eyes. Opening my eyes seemed to open my brain at the same time, and all the pain in the world flooded viciously through my body. I didn't have any stomach. It had been reduced to twisted knots of raw flesh. The inside of my mouth, and all the way down my throat, tasted and felt like rum-soaked leather. When I tried to see out of my eyes, half a dozen gremlins drew multicolored curtains up and down so fast that it was like swimming through a liquid rainbow.

I closed my eyes again and tried desperately to force myself back into that blissful state of unconsciousness, but it wouldn't work at all. A mumbo-jumbo murmur of voices coming from all sides finally pried my eyes open again. The multicolored curtains had been stored away, praise Allah, and I was able to see a few other things. All of them made no sense at all, and a little icy chill began to crawl up and down my backbone. I was on a bed in a long narrow room. There were other beds along each side of the wall, and in every bed there was somebody. Each somebody a man. All wore makeshift night shirts, and when I looked down my nose I saw that I was wearing one, too. And just me and my bare skin underneath. A chair beside the head of my bed didn't have a stitch of clothing hanging on it.

Crazy fear drove two quick hard ones to the pit of my belly, and I sat up in bed. Nobody looked my way. The others, who were not sleeping, or pretending to sleep, were either sitting on the edge of the beds heads in hands, or just sitting and staring silly-faced off into space. I opened my mouth to ask the most important question in the world for me at the moment. Just at that instant, though, a door I hadn't yet noticed swung open and a tall, skinny lad came gliding inside. He wore white pants and a three-quarter-length white smock.

He also wore glasses, and his face was expressionless as the bottom of the hull of the *Queen Mary*. He came right over to my bed.

'How do you feel?' he wanted to know. 'Do you hurt much?'

Instead of answering, I asked the important question right then and there. 'Where am I?'

'Morgan Hospital,' he replied. Then maybe as an afterthought, 'The alcoholic ward.'

'*What?*'

The way I got that out woke up everybody who was really asleep. The lad in white frowned and half lifted a hand.

'Take it easy,' he said quietly. 'Take it easy. What's your name?'

'Barnes, Gerry Barnes,' I replied automatically. Then also automatically I added, 'I'm a private detective.'

The frown went away as he lifted his brows a little. His lips twitched a little. 'Really?' he murmured.

'Definitely!' I snapped, or thought I snapped at him. 'Now let's have it! How did I get here, and where are my clothes?

What's the big idea, anyway?'

'*You*,' he replied, as though I should have known. 'We're only helping you. Last night you were found half in and half out of the East River, down by Ninety-Sixth. Some kid found you and called a cop. Fellows like you are our job. We went and got you. You were banged up some, but not much. You reeked to high heaven of the stuff. You must have fallen from the wall there. So we brought you here. We're city-operated, you know. Now, if you'll just . . . '

'My clothes!' I cut in as the icy things began to crawl up and down my spine again. 'You must have searched the pockets and found . . . '

His shaking head stopped me.

'We found nothing,' he said. 'Not even a handkerchief. I guess you were probably rolled where you'd passed but, and then pushed over the wall.'

'Look,' I said as calmly as I could, 'you got the wrong party this time. Just the same, though, I thank you for all you did. And I'll do more than that, as soon as I get home. I'll add a nice little check to my thanks. Now go get my clothes, will you? I want to get out of here. I have some things to do.'

'Sorry,' he said, with the nearest thing to a smile he could muster up. 'Against the rules. However, if there's somebody who can come here to identify you, and vouch for you, we might . . . ?'

'Fair enough!' I interrupted. 'Go phone . . . '

A horrible thought made me snap my mouth shut. I had been on the point of telling him to phone Paula, when I realized she was the last person in the world I wanted to come to that place and identify me. Definitely I would then be trapped. I mean, I would most certainly have to marry the woman in exchange for her on-a-stack-of-Bibles promise never to rib me either in public or in private. No, definitely not Paula. And then I got a bright idea. It would not only put fire under this lad in white, but maybe it would help me square off a few things that were bothering my brains. At least the part that had come up off the floor and was functioning after a fashion.

'Phone the Homicide Bureau,' I told him. 'Get Lieutenant Bierman on the wire, and tell him Gerry Barnes is here, and would like him to come here, but fast!'

Yes, it certainly jolted him. The way to take all in his stride that he had learned in medical school, left him without a single prop. He stiffened, and gulped. And then he gaped.

'Lieutenant Bierman, of *Homicide*?' he managed to get out. 'Then . . . then you really *are* a private detective?'

I looked sadly at the shafts of warm sunlight slanting through the row of windows in back of me.

'Yeah,' I grunted. 'Up until now, I thought I was. Hurry it up, will you?'

He turned around and went away. I sank back on the pillow, and closed my eyes, and tried not to think. The whole thing was certainly messed up. I didn't even know what team we were playing, let alone the score. All I knew was that somehow I had been tagged 'it.' But I couldn't see or even think of anybody to tag in turn.

Five of the most terrible minutes in my life dragged by, and then the door swung open and he came back. He had my shoes in one hand, and the rest of my clothes over the other arm. He placed the lot on the chair by the head of my bed, and gave me a funny look.

'Lieutenant Bierman seemed quite excited,' he said. 'He told me to tell you that he was on his way here how.'

I nodded and made no comment. The lad was as nervously eager as a lassie on her wedding night, but I just let him fight it out by himself. I grabbed my clothes and went through all the pockets. Out of everyone, I pulled nothing but my hand. Cleaned, but good. Even the underwear, shirt, and suit labels had been ripped out. That sent a shudder through me as I realized the meaning behind it. News-paper headlines formed in my brain. Bloated body fished out of the Narrows! Being carried out to sea by the tide! Identification impossible! Etc. But why? That sixty-four-dollar question stumped me for the moment. Why had those unseen crumbs that had belted me around wanted to see me dead for keeps? They'd known from my crack that I knew which one of them had garroted DeFoe? Maybe. My head ached so much, though, I dropped it, and began getting into my clothes.

Bierman must have set some kind of a speed record, because he came barging through the door just as I was slipping into my jacket. He gave me one look, and then switched his eyes to my skinny guardian's face.

'I'm Lieutenant Bierman,' he clipped out. 'I spoke to Dr. Small downstairs. I'll take it from here.'

'Of course, Lieutenant, of course.' The lad in white gulped, but he didn't move an inch.

Bierman stepped by him and took a good look at me. Maybe my eyesight wasn't up to par yet, but I didn't see the slightest sign of sympathy in his eyes.

'Can you navigate under your own power, Barnes?' he wanted to know.

'Sure,' I told him. 'Let's go.'

'Yeah,' he echoed, and I guess habit made him take one of my arms. 'Let's go.'

Out in front his car was waiting, with his right hand, Sergeant Goff, behind the wheel. Goff looked me over good as we walked over and climbed in. What he thought I didn't guess, or try. I got in back with Bierman at my heels, and then gave him a crooked grin.

'We've got lots of things to talk about, Lieutenant,' I said, 'but in my condition I'd never be able to say a word down at Centre Street. Tell you what. Come to my place, and we'll go over it all while I clean up, and eat. As I recall, it hasn't been since breakfast yesterday. You could do with a bite yourself, couldn't you? And Sergeant Goff? I'll send down for it. For free, of course.'

A lot of words, and a couple of times Bierman made as though to cut in, but he didn't. I guess it was how I must have looked that decided things for him. Could have been, though, that he was hungry, too.

'All right, Goff,' he said, and leaned back on the cushions. 'His apartment.'

10

Lieutenant Frank Bierman can be one of the toughest, meanest, and nastiest guys in the world when it suits him. But I will say this much for him. He can also be one of the nicest guys in the world when he's in the mood. And, praise be, he was in that mood when we three drove away from the Morgan Hospital. And what's more, he stayed in that mood until I had showered, shaved, dressed in fresh clothes, and was sitting down to a mess of food, and he and Goff to a cup of coffee. There the nice mood folded up and hurried away.

'All right, Barnes,' he said, tight-lipped. 'The beginning is a good place to start. And I might mention I want all of it. Whether you think so or not, you could be in a very unpleasant spot right now.'

I shot him a quick look over the top of a toasted English muffin. 'Meaning just what?' I wanted to know.

He waved it away with a gesture.

'Later, perhaps,' he said. 'Right now I'm just listening.'

I let him listen and not hear a thing from me for a couple of minutes. A brace of straight shots before sitting down to eat had helped me a lot, but not enough. I mean, I was still all mixed up about almost everything. A couple of items I had pinned down right where I wanted them. But I certainly wasn't going to tell Bierman about them. So where to begin? I decided that the place where I'd stepped into that taxi in front of Goldilocks' apartment building and had gone bye-bye would be the best.

So I told him all about it. Every single detail that I could remember. I even made that room conversation word for word as near as I could. No, not because I wanted to unburden myself completely for his sake. Simply because I wanted to get his reaction to it. He listened right through to the end without a change of expression. He didn't even look at me more than a couple of times. And then only flash glances. His coffee, cream, and sugar seemed to hold him mesmerized. But when I was finished he reached into an inner pocket and pulled out a little notebook. He flipped three or four pages, then held it and looked at me.

'When you left your office, you met somebody on the sidewalk,' he said. 'You went to the Biltmore cocktail lounge with him. Who was he?'

'A client,' I said. And that certainly was no lie now.

'What kind of a client?' he barked a little. 'Don't try and get fancy with me, Barnes!'

He shouldn't have said that. Not that I was planning to tell him. Not by a damn sight. He just shouldn't have said it to me with my pounding head, and all the six hundred other pains.

'That isn't in the rules, Bierman,' I told him flatly. 'You know it, too. He was a client on his way up to see me. You'd tossed me out of my own office so I took him to the Biltmore. We talked our business there. Your shadow probably saw him hand me my retainer.'

Bierman grunted, cleared his throat, and took another look at his notebook.

'From the Biltmore, you went to call on Miss Grant,' he said.

'She *isn't* a client,' I said with a faint grin. 'And what we talked about was strictly private.'

He glanced at me and suddenly I felt oddly funny. Something in his eyes. I guess you could call it that they tightened up a little at the corners.

'Anything wrong in visiting Paula?' I demanded.

'Miss Grant is a very fine woman,' he said, and went back to his notebook.

I was on the point of digging around a little for exactly what he meant, but he didn't give me a chance.

'From her apartment, you went to Radio City,' he said. Then, as the ghost of a pleased grin flitted across his face, he went on, 'You thought you'd shaken your tail, and took a cab to a Park Avenue address. The apartment of a Miss Zara Zaralis, to be exact. Check?'

'Check,' I said. Then, because I really meant it, 'Your man is good, Bierman. He deserves a promotion.'

Bierman acted as though I hadn't even

spoken. He was looking at me, and maybe through me, too. 'This one I *do* want answered, Barnes,' he said evenly. 'What did you see the Zaralis woman about?'

The way he said it made me mad. But with Bierman, a very, very little can make me mad. Anyway, I took my time in answering.

'I met her at the Rankins' party,' I said. 'She invited me to drop by for a drink sometime. So I did. We just talked about this and that for a while. Not long, as your shadow probably told you. By the way, you'd better switch shadows. I could spot him a mile away now. Tall, skinny, and a razor face. He . . . '

Bierman's slightly blank look and the start of his head shake stopped me.

'No?' I said, and it was a trifle weak.

'No, so you didn't spot him,' he told me. 'You must have seen somebody else.'

I looked hard at Bierman, trying to figure if it was on the level. 'That's straight?' I blurted out. 'I really want to know, Bierman, because it was the tall skinny guy I was trying to shake.'

'Somebody else,' he replied bluntly.

'Any idea who could have put him on your heels?'

I tried to make him see I was thinking hard on that one. 'No,' I finally said with a slow shake of my head. 'Unless it could have been the lad who slipped the wire necklace on DeFoe. What's new on that, anyway?'

'First things first,' Bierman brushed it aside. 'Did you have a fight with that Zaralis woman?'

The question came so unexpectedly that I couldn't control my start. The bit of fried egg on my fork stopped cold halfway to my mouth, slipped off and dropped back onto the plate.

'A fight?' I echoed sharply. 'Hell, no! It was completely the other way, if you get me. And now it's my turn. Where in hell was your smart shadow when I stepped into that cab and got my head caved in?'

I guess Bierman had been expecting that question, and dreading it. His face went a dull red, and he quickly looked the other way.

'He won't shadow anybody else for a long time,' he said grimly. 'He took time out to phone me and let me know where you were. It was during his call you disappeared. What do you know about that Zaralis dame?'

'Little or nothing,' I told him truthfully. 'Cute, with certain atomic qualities. And I wouldn't be surprised if she's a whole lot smarter than she looks and acts. But mind telling me why you are so interested in her?'

'For several reasons,' he replied in an offhand manner. 'One of them being that her apartment is in René DeFoe's name. Did you know that?'

That one caught me bull's eye dead center. So it was a few seconds before I could even shake my head.

'From the looks I figured it was somebody with dough,' I said. 'But I didn't have the faintest idea who. Wait a minute! You think . . . ?' I let it stay right there, and looked at him. He shrugged and looked right back at me.

'A thought for consideration,' he finally grunted. 'The old saying, dynamite comes in small packages. No doubt you wrestled a bit, Barnes. Would you say her hands were strong enough to garrote a guy she didn't like?'

I resented his inference, but I was too busy thinking new thoughts to take issue. Goldilocks was full of steel springs, even though she was pint-sized. But that didn't mean too much to me. When it comes to garroting, strength isn't all of it. Perfect surprise, and timing, have a whole lot more to do with your degree of success. Goldilocks? Maybe. Then again, maybe not.

'I don't think so, Bierman,' I said slowly. 'But don't take my word for it. About DeFoe . . . '

'No, stay on the track!' he cut me off. 'When would you say you left her place?'

'One o'clock, but maybe it was closer to two,' I replied. 'I know it was time for lunch. Why?'

He glanced at his notebook again. 'The Morgan Hospital people took you in about half after midnight,' he said. 'Out cold, and stinking, they told me. What did these mysterious attackers do? Crown you with a full bottle of liquor? You were soaked in the stuff, they told me.'

'Don't forget, plenty beaten up too,' I said, and touched a couple of still sore spots on my face. Then, suddenly real mad, I blasted out, 'Look, Bierman, do you think I made that up? Because if you do, you're a — '

'Keep your shirt on, Barnes!' he cut in on me. 'Flying off the handle gets both of us nowhere. I gave you a break, coming here. I can take that back any time I want to.'

I looked at Sergeant Goff, who hadn't spoken a single word. He had just sipped his coffee and set both ears at full cock. He looked at me with a look that told me he was definitely on Bierman's side. I forced myself to cool down, and swallow what was left of my wrath.

'Sorry,' I mumbled into my coffee cup. 'But I really got put through the hoops last night. It rasps to find out you think different.'

'Nobody could look at your face and think different,' Bierman said dryly. 'I'm not questioning that. But I am questioning by whom!'

'I told you, I don't know,' I replied, still

115

keeping the lid on my anger. 'I was blindfolded and tied up. There were three of them, as I explained. I have a hunch one was the lad who tailed me along with your man. But that's only a hunch. I'd never heard his voice before, but I'll recognize it next time . . . if there is a next time. Which I hope!'

Bierman gave a grunt, and started fiddling with his coffee spoon while he stared off into space. In some way that was as a little secret signal for me to start feeling uneasy, and not at all certain of how firm the ground was where I was standing. Every one of my questions, practically, Bierman had waved to one side. He didn't have to send me a special delivery to tell me that he was holding something back. Something that was going to knock me for four bases when it struck. I watched him play with that damn coffee spoon, and stare at nothing at all, for two full minutes. Then:

'All right,' I said evenly. 'I'm all sweaty. So pop whatever you plan to pop.'

He dropped the spoon in the saucer, and lowered his eyes to mine. 'Let's say you left there at two o'clock,' he said. 'At twelve-thirty, the Morgan people had you. Ten hours and a half. That's a lot of hours.'

'That's right, a lot of hours,' I agreed. 'And I might add, I don't think I was conscious in that room for more than half an hour. Call it ten hours even. And I can't account for so much as a minute of one of them. So?'

Bierman's eyes tightened, and frosted. 'Sure you didn't have a scrap with that Zaralis woman, Barnes?' he shot at me. 'A scrap, and maybe went back later to . . . finish it?'

Red rage surged up in me, but it didn't get to the top. I was suddenly ice cold all over. I looked at Bierman for quick confirmation of what I was thinking, but there was nothing but frost in his eyes. I swallowed and licked my lips.

'Not then, or even later,' I said, and my voice was hollow. 'What happened? You mean she's . . . someone . . . ?' My words were getting so mixed up I stopped them altogether. I don't know why, but I came close to fainting with relief when I saw

Bierman shake his head.

'No,' he said. 'But it was almost close enough to be. A woman in the apartment next to hers heard her screams. She called downstairs, and they called us. I happened to take the call, and when I heard the name I went along. We had to break open the door. She was on the floor of that over-furnished sunken living room. She had been beaten up some, but mostly scratched. The neck and arms, and a couple of good ones on the side of her face. It took us about ten minutes to bring her to.'

'And then what?' I asked, certain that he had purposely stopped. 'Dammit! What did she tell you?'

Bierman growled in his throat and gave a chew of his lower lip. 'Not very much,' he said. 'She said she answered the door ring, and somebody threw pepper in her face, and then came at her. She couldn't see, and she had her hands full scrapping. Couldn't even tell if it was man or woman. The last she remembers is screaming for help. Nuts! She knew who it was. Goddammit, she must have. But she swore not. For my money, she lies like hell.'

A bit of memory had tinkled in the back of my head, and the room was slowly beginning to go round and round. Ice water was in my stomach, and with each revolution of the room, some of that ice water splashed up over my heart to freeze there into ice.

'What time was this?' I asked.

'Eleven thirty-five the call came in,' he said. 'We got there at eleven forty-five. Why?'

I didn't answer. I didn't even try to answer, because I couldn't have. The bit of memory was tinkling again. I was remembering how Paula had not believed my telephone gag ... how I had supposedly made a date with the little blonde fireball for eleven thirty. A man usually leads with his fists, but women always lead with their fingernails!

11

'Snap out of it, Barnes! I'm waiting. *Why?* A dummy can see you're stalling! Why are you so interested in the time?'

'I don't know that I am, for sure,' I said slowly. 'There's . . . Dammit, I don't know!'

'You haven't a thing on me!' Bierman clipped out. 'What do you mean, you don't know?'

It was an act, of course, so I tried to make it as good as I could. I frowned at him, and through him, and touched one hand to my head.

'It's like there's something about it I should remember, but can't,' I said. 'Maybe something I heard one of them say in that room last night. Bierman, the time, eleven thirty, clicks with me on something. But, so help me, I don't know what. Maybe it'll come later.'

'Yes, maybe,' he murmured, and handed me a keen look. 'Now, about this

DeFoe. You didn't tell me everything yesterday when I walked in on you.'

I grinned right at him. 'And certainly neither did you,' I parried. 'That saying you'd dropped in to say hello wasn't even a try, Bierman. A very obvious fib.'

He looked mad, and then he looked slightly hurt. And then it seemed to strike him funny, because he laughed a little.

'You private ops are really something,' he said eventually. 'Whenever one of you beats us to the tape on a case, you think we silently swear everlasting vengeance. You're crazy, did you know it?'

'Some of my best friends have said those very words to me,' I replied politely.

He gave a shake of his head and a wave of his hand. 'I was speaking generally, not personally,' he said. 'You won't believe it, Barnes, but I actually *did* drop around just to see how things were.'

I stared at him for the telltale twinkle, but there was none. 'Straight?' I demanded.

'On the level,' he assured me. 'Word of honor. Dammit, Barnes, why can't . . . ?' He shrugged and let it go. So did I, without shrugging. I was not a little amazed to say the least.

'Well, that's certainly a coincidence I'll have to tell my grandchildren about,' I murmured.

'Do that!' Bierman grunted, and put away his little notebook. 'Now, back to DeFoe. You can tell me now the parts you left out.'

'If I left anything out, it was because it wasn't important,' I said dryly. 'Also, I recall getting the bum's rush. What the hell did you expect, anyway?'

He wasn't riled even a little bit. 'I found out all about that fight, Barnes,' he said quietly.

'Wrong,' I said with a snorting laugh. 'Neither of them threw a punch.'

'I know that,' he said smoothly. 'But *you* did. Several of them. At DeFoe!'

'Who told you that?' I snapped.

'My crystal ball, of course,' he murmured with a grin.

'Then trade it in,' I suggested. 'Your crystal ball lies like hell!'

'So?'

'So,' I echoed, 'I didn't throw any punches. I simply threw a couple of nice body blocks to keep DeFoe from maybe killing Cardeur right then and there. I told you I helped break it up. Sorry, pal, I'm not your man. Besides, garroting is too fancy for me. When do I get my check back? The one he made out to me?'

'Maybe when you tell me *why* he made it out,' Bierman said.

I shook my head and gave a mock heavy sigh. 'Then I'll never get it, because I honestly don't know the answer to that one.'

Bierman didn't say anything for a long minute. He used it up inspecting me as though I was something very rare, and just a little unbelievable. Finally he lowered his gaze to his coffee cup and stuck his lower lip way out.

'I believe you, Barnes,' he said quietly. 'This once I really do.'

'Thanks,' I said dryly. And then I softened a bit. 'For once that's the truth, Bierman. I simply haven't the faintest. I'll even go a step further than that. I haven't the faintest idea about anything that's happened. Truthfully, I wish to hell I'd never gone near the Rankins' party. I didn't want to, as it was.'

A fair length of silence followed my last words. Bierman seemed a thousand miles away, and I certainly wished I were. Then I asked a question about the thing that was bothering me most. At least at the moment.

'Putting your crystal ball to one side, Bierman,' I said, 'just where did you hear the details about the almost-scrap between DeFoe and Cardeur?'

The deadly serious look on his face floated away. He leaned forward and grinned. Very cat-at-canary stuff, and twice as corny. 'You'd never guess in a million years,' he said.

I looked at him and started to open my mouth. Then I closed my mouth, but still looked at him. It was incredible, absolutely impossible. But of course I knew darn well it was true. As I have mentioned more than once, there are very few people who can outsmart Lieutenant Frank Bierman, and no one I've ever met who can outthink him.

'Paula Grant?' I asked, and it cost me a tremendous effort.

'Miss Grant.' He nodded. 'You said she'd been at the party, so I dropped around for a chat. She . . . ' He paused, and grinned a little, the louse! 'She didn't seem in the mood to talk about you, Barnes,' he said. 'Nice things about you, I mean. I wouldn't get too sore about it, though, if I were you. When a woman's sore, she doesn't think along very logical lines. She told me about your sending this DeFoe for the count.'

'Any other fairy tales?' I asked.

He shook his head and made a face. 'No,' he said with a touch of regret. 'Not even why she was sore at you. I'd kind of like to know, though. Why was she?'

'Never ask a guy about his best girl's moods, Bierman,' I said solemnly. 'He can't even figure them out for himself. But thanks for telling me it was Paula.'

That straightened him up fast.

'Why?' he demanded.

'I thought it was the Zaralis dame,' I lied. Then, with what I thought was a very snappy leer, 'She was at that party, too, as you probably know. And yesterday noon she definitely didn't want me to leave so

125

soon. Women are strange, my friend.'

He grunted as though he wasn't interested. He got to his feet and started reaching for his hat. For me, our little chit-chat hadn't even begun.

'Have one more cup,' I invited. 'Better still, I'll send down for some hot.'

He shook his head and lifted a hand that held me in my chair. 'No thanks, Barnes. Some other time, maybe. Right now . . . '

'Right now, how about answering a couple of my questions?' I cut in quickly. 'As suspect number one, I'm due a little consideration.'

'Nuts!' he growled. 'About being any kind of a suspect, I mean. And maybe I say that with sorrow, too. Well, what do you want to know?'

'For one thing, all about DeFoe,' I replied quickly. 'What have you found out? And what progress, if any?'

'In a word, nothing,' he said. 'At least nothing that can help us very much. Just the usual things you find in a murdered man's pockets. Name, pieces of identification, a paid hotel bill where he was staying, a couple of addresses here in New York, and a couple of dozen European addresses.'

Don't ask me why, but I pricked up my ears at that last. 'What kind of European addresses?' I asked.

He looked at me with faint scorn. 'Keep it clean,' he grunted. 'There wasn't a single woman's name in the little book. Black, too, but it wasn't that kind of a little black book.'

I grinned the disappointed wolf by way of playing along with that dumb bit of conclusion-jumping on Bierman's part. 'Then what kind of addresses were they?' I asked.

He shrugged as though to say: Why bother asking that? 'Business houses, they struck me,' he replied. 'London, Paris, Amsterdam, Antwerp, and a few others. They didn't tell me what lines he was representing, though. Nor did a good search of his hotel room tell us anything, either. Frankly, just another rich business-man.'

That last made me prick up my ears the second time.

'Rich?' I echoed. 'What do you mean by that?'

He gave me a very secretive smile. 'Banks are always glad to cooperate with the recognized law,' he said in a voice just brimming with pointed meaning. 'Ten days ago he opened an account in that bank your check was drawn on. For fifty thousand. Thirty of it in American Victory Bonds not six months old, and the rest in cash. The war was certainly hard on him!'

I nodded to show I got exactly what he meant, but it had more or less been words in and out of my ears. Despite the beating the Barnes brain had stumbled through, it was now working fast and furiously to make up for lost time. In fact, a couple of other questions I had wanted very much to ask Bierman didn't even seem worth the asking now. At any rate, I thought I could postpone the asking for an indefinite period of time. Right now, the thing I wanted most was Bierman's and Goff's company no longer. I gave a puzzled shake of my head, pushed away my plate with a gesture that I was through, and got onto my own feet.

'Well, we certainly are starting from scratch,' I said with a pale smile. 'What we both know doesn't even make a loud foul. We'll just have to keep pitching, that's all.'

Bierman put on his hat, gave it a couple of tugs, and then studied me intently a moment from underneath its brim.

'Yes, to be sure,' he murmured. 'But I think I'd like to know what kind of stuff you're going to throw, beginning with when Goff and I blow out of here. Wouldn't tell, would you, by any chance?'

I laughed along with that and made a gesture he could take any one of a dozen ways.

'I wish I knew myself, Bierman,' I said. 'Seems like the only hope I've got is to tramp the streets of New York listening for a reedy voice I'll recognize. If and when I do, I'll begin from there.'

Bierman grunted, and half jerked his head at Goff. Then he looked at me again. Smiling at me, but only with his lips.

'Do that,' he said. 'And maybe you'll get in touch with me . . . if and when?'

I widened my eyes, and looked surprised. 'No shadow?' I asked.

He motioned to Goff again, and the pair of them moved toward the door. 'I'll make up my mind on that later,' he said. 'But probably not. You're much too smart for even me, Barnes.'

And with that the two of them went out the door, and closed it shut. I stared at the closed door, and pondered deeply on just who had won, and who had lost. I decided to call it a draw, and went over to the telephone on my living room desk.

12

It took about five minutes of my dialing to convince me that Paula wasn't home, and that was why she didn't answer the phone. I thought of calling a couple of places she might be, but finally decided against it. Considering this and that, I really didn't want to see her that bad, yet.

So I called downstairs for a waiter to come up and clear away the victual debris. And then I made an after-brunch drink and settled in my favorite chair to really think things over. Ten minutes ago the whole thing had been nothing less than a mess. And nothing more, too, as far as that went. But now a tiny thought was growing by leaps and bounds inside my head. When I looked at it closely, I told myself that I was nuts. I mean, I wasn't writing a murder story. I was living one. And one of the most cockeyed, too, that anyone would ever want to live.

Nevertheless, the little thought grew

and grew. So to follow it along, I went to the phone again and made a couple of long-distance calls to Washington, D. C. to a couple of old friends who had jobs in places where people knew a whole lot of things that the public didn't. Both of them tried to skip rope when I asked some slightly delicate questions. But they finally said they would think those questions over, and maybe let me know. *Maybe!* For the time being, that was okay by me. The way they had skipped rope made me feel pretty sure I was beginning to travel along the right track.

When I finally hung up, I wished very much that I could turn myself into the Invisible Man. Then I could whisk away down to Bierman's Center Street office and pick up that little black book he had found on DeFoe. That for me was the thing around which everything else was spinning.

However, even in the OSS they didn't teach us how to become the Invisible Man, so getting the little black book that way was out. I would have to think up a better way. And with Bierman and his pals running interference for that book, the way I thought up would have to be damn good.

So I decided on another line of action. One that was slightly long overdue, as a matter of fact. I didn't have it anymore, but I had been handed fifteen hundred bucks to find a certain Maurice Cardeur. It seemed about time I made an effort to earn what I had been paid, but didn't have. I finished my drink, got my hat and went down to the street. If Bierman had left a shadow, I didn't see him. I hailed a cab and rode around town for half an hour or so. But not in the same cab. I changed four times. And when I finally gave the last cabby the Hotel Green address on East Seventeenth Street, I was dead sure that any and all tails had been ditched but good. If not, then I'd better get out of the detecting business and just enjoy the dough a dear departed uncle had left me. And which, by the way, had made it possible for me to realize a life-long dream and get into the detecting business in the first place.

If you were walking very fast, and

thinking of something else, you'd go right by the Hotel Green without even seeing it. The sign, a very small one, was practically lost in a mass of other signs that told you where to buy furniture, watches, sport clothes, and a whole lot of other items. The lobby was one flight up. You reached it by a narrow stairway that angled up from the sidewalk.

The lobby was a very poor excuse for such. And the bald-headed, jaundice-skinned little geezer in back of the desk looked like something ready to go to the morgue. He was sound asleep, and I had to bang the little punch bell three times before he woke up. Or perhaps condescended to open his mottled oyster eyes. He looked at me with all the excited interest of a man watching a fly crawl up the wall.

'Yeah?' he lisped through the opening made by two missing upper front teeth.

'Mr. Maurice Cardeur,' I said. 'What's his room number?'

The little geezer's eyes tightened as he shook his head. 'Ain't in his room,' he said.

I looked sorry, and a little vexed. I also glanced at my wristwatch. 'When will he ever be on time?' I mumbled as though to myself. Then to him, with a sigh, 'I'll wait for him in his room. What was the number?'

'Ain't in his room,' he repeated. Then, maybe to make certain I got it right, he added, 'Ain't been in his room for a couple of days and nights now.'

'Oh, I know that,' I said with a gesture. 'He had to run up to Albany. Saw him just before he left. We made an appointment to meet here this noon. It's all right. Just show me his room, and . . . '

'Nope!' he cut in on me. 'Against the rules. Besides, you ain't kidding nobody, mister.'

'How's that?' I echoed, and didn't have much trouble looking surprised.

'That's what I said!' he declared. 'You, and all them others, ain't kidding nobody. I tell you he ain't in, and he ain't. If you feel like waiting, there's a chair right there behind you.'

My first reaction was to take a good handful of the front of his shirt and see if

I could shake him loose from it. Of course, though, I curbed that idea as soon as it was born. I also thought of letting him see my holstered gun (I had carefully strapped it in place before leaving my apartment) plus a flash at my spare detective badge I had taken out of my bureau drawer. But that urge I pushed away, too. No doubt the little geezer would scare easily, but I decided there was a much better way to get cooperation. A way as old as the hills. I slipped my hand into my pocket.

'Thanks, I guess I will,' I said.

As I turned I slid the five-dollar bill on the lobby desk and took my hand away. Then I went over and sat down. He looked at the money, and then at me. Suspicion stood out on his face like a rash.

'For free,' I said, and lighted a cigarette.

When I looked up from lighting it, the five-dollar bill was gone, and he was still looking at me. I frowned a little, and shook my head.

'There's no catch,' I said. Then with a

wink, I added, 'If there was, I'd tell you that bill had some sisters and brothers . . . which it has.'

While he mulled that over, I took a forced interest in the dingy, gloomy surroundings. When you added it all up, it still came out the same. It was just the lobby of a third-rate flea trap. Just that and nothing more, or less. When I glanced casually his way, the suspicious rash had faded away. If you could call it such, there was almost a gleam of polite interest in his eyes. And just the ghost of a smile on his lips.

'Well, you're different from them others, mister,' he said. 'I'll say that much for you.'

'Others?' I murmured, and let my brows climb. 'Many of them?'

'Four or five,' he replied. 'But not all at once.'

'Any women?' I asked, and yawned.

'Dames?' he echoed, startled. 'Nope. There was a dame, though. Before he took this trip you was telling me about, I mean. But each time *she* come, he was *in*! We ain't got too many rules here, y'know.'

He winked, and I winked back . . . with a leer.

'Know just what you mean, buddy,' I told him. 'Fact is, I know her well. A little bundle of gold leaf. Right?'

His chuckle sounded like water going down the drain. 'Right!' he agreed. 'Cute little bit, too. Wouldn't mind myself . . . if I was twenty years younger.'

We both laughed hard at that. We were becoming pals very fast. I speeded things up by wandering over and sliding another bill toward him. This one was a ten.

'When a guy has a million other things to do, it's hell just to wait around,' I grunted. 'Cardeur always keeps a bottle in his room. Maybe you and I could find it, huh?'

He liked that suggestion very much. He liked it so much he turned and took a key off one of a dozen hooks. When he turned back front, he was grinning.

'You must be a good friend of his if you know that, mister,' he said. 'Come on. Hell with the rules. I'm making this a new one.'

It had all been so simple I wanted to laugh. But I didn't. I had only got to second. It was still a long way to home. As I followed him up two flights, and along a gloomy tunnel toward the rear of the building, I wondered how much it would cost me when we found there wasn't any bottle in Cardeur's room. I mean, how much to have the little geezer leave me there and go back to his hole?

However, I could have saved myself all that wondering. He stopped in front of the end door on the left, unlocked it with the key, and pushed the door open. The light inside the room wasn't much better than the light in the tunnel that was a hallway. But it was enough for both of us.

'Jesus Christ!' he shrilled. 'What the hell?'

I stepped around him and into the room. Into what once had been a room, I mean. It wasn't a room now, though. True, there were four walls, a ceiling, and a floor, but there it ceased to bear any kind of a resemblance. In a single sentence, it looked like a B-29 had made a forced landing in the place. Everything — chairs, table, bureau, suitcases, bedclothes, mattress, and every-thing else — was scattered all over the room. The pillows of the bed had been ripped open, and the whole business was covered with a layer of feathers. The mattress, too, had been ripped, and half a dozen coiled springs were popped up out of it like small shrubs through the snow. I have seen rooms turned upside down in my time, but this one had not only been turned upside down, it had been turned inside out.

'That dirty bastard! That no-good, stinking, dirty bastard!' The little geezer stood right where he'd stopped. His eyes were dinner plates, and the cuss words came off his lips slowly, deliberately, and vehemently.

'Who is?' I asked sharply. 'You mean Cardeur?'

He stopped swearing long enough to look at me and shake his head. 'Christ, there goes my job. And for five bucks. For a lousy five bucks. Goddamn that . . . '

'Skip it!' I cut in on him. 'If it wasn't Cardeur, then who was it?'

'Dunno!' he grated. 'But he was a lousy, stinking . . . '

The ten-dollar bill in my hand stopped

him just as neatly as though I'd pushed my fist down his throat. He didn't reach for it, though. He looked at me and screwed up one eye.

'Yeah? You make them things, mister?'

'Straight from the mint,' I told him. 'I always pay for anything I buy. Want to do a little business? This could help if you do lose your job.'

He took his screwed-up eyes off me long enough to sweep the room around once. And make up his mind. 'What do you want to buy, mister?' he asked.

I reached over and tucked the ten in his shirt pocket. He made no movement to pull back. 'Cardeur's visitors,' I said. 'Since he went to Albany. Five, you said?'

'Five, I think,' he grunted with a frown. 'Could be four, maybe. I don't pay much attention who comes and goes in this dump. Maybe one of them came back twice.'

'Describe them,' I said.

'Huh, mister?'

'Tell me what they looked like.'

He frowned, scratched his bald head, and then shook it. 'None was a dame,' he finally said. 'Just guys, that's all. I said I don't pay much attention. Take the sawbuck back, mister.'

I stayed his hand with my own. 'Keep it,' I said. 'Maybe you can tell me this. When was the last one here?'

'Yesterday afternoon,' he said after a period of concentrated thought. 'Yeah, about the middle of the afternoon. And here's something else. Yeah. That guy had come once before, too. Seems like it was night before last, I think. But I don't pay much attention. Guys and dames. They come and go in this fleabag.'

I nodded, and caught his eye, and held it. 'And the last one to come you let in here for five bucks,' I shot at him. 'How long was he in here?'

He looked as though he was going to get real mad. He even half-pulled my ten dollars from his shirt pocket. But maybe the feel of crisp new money was too much for him. He poked it back in, and nodded.

'Yeah,' he said. Then heavily, 'For a lousy five . . . and my job.'

'You can get another,' I said easily.

'Plenty of jobs these days. Now here's ten to mate that one in your shirt pocket. Yours, if you think hard. Real hard, understand?'

He looked at me for a long moment. Then his lips twitched. 'I'm thinking, mister,' he said. 'Real hard.'

'The lad who did this,' I said, and waved my hand at the mess. 'What did *he* look like?'

Whether he was really thinking hard, or just stalling while he made something up, I couldn't tell by watching him. So I just waited with my right hand out a little, and the ten-dollar bill showing very plainly. He took a minute, or maybe a minute and a half. Then he gave me the description. Not much. Little more than a brief thumbnail sketch. But it was enough for me. He had not been stalling. He had actually been thinking real hard.

The man he described was Gordon Parrish!

13

Was that knowledge startling? In a way, yes. And in a way, no. I mean, I had a hunch Parrish had done the room blitz job. What I thought about when the little geezer stopped talking was whether or not proof that my hunch was correct was worth thirty-five bucks of my money. I still couldn't make up my mind when he pulled me back from my thought trance.

'That help any?' he asked, but his eyes were focused on the bill still in my right hand.

'Maybe,' I said, and gave it to him. 'Sure you can't remember what the others looked like?'

He shook his head firmly. 'Straight, mister,' he said. 'You're a right guy, and if I could I sure would. But I can't. They was just guys with clothes on. The last one, though, anybody would half remember at least. On account of that mug of his. But the others? Nope.'

Well, that seemed to be that. For what it was worth. One thing, though, wouldn't be worth a dime, not to mention a waste of time and effort. I mean, my searching the room. Whatever Parrish had been looking for, either he had found it or he hadn't found it. If the latter, then I certainly wouldn't even get to first, because I'd carry the handicap of not knowing what the devil it was.

I turned to walk out of the room, but suddenly a screwy sort of invisible force seemed to make me stop and turn around again. I had the impression all at once that something was screaming out loud for attention. What, I hadn't the faintest. My imagination was just running wild, I decided. That didn't help any, though. Something held me there, as though both my shoes were nailed to the floor.

I stood there so long just staring at the mess in the room that the bald-headed little geezer started shifting from one foot to the other, and shooting me snap looks that became increasingly filled with fear-quaking apprehension. Finally he couldn't stand it any longer.

'What's the matter, mister?' he squeaked out. 'You think I been stringing you, huh? Honest to God . . . '

I shook my head to stop him. 'Forget it,' I grunted without looking at him. 'The dough is all yours. But I could do with a favor.'

'Yeah?'

I waved one hand to include the whole room, and then turned to give him the steady eye. He started to tremble a little, and I let him tremble.

'There's something screwy about this,' I said evenly. 'Very screwy. Who would want anything they could find in this dump?'

'Not me,' he said. 'I wouldn't even give a buck for the whole lousy building. But why did that stinking louse wreck the joint?'

I wished that I could answer that question to my own satisfaction. I couldn't, though, so I answered it with a shrug and a half-shake of my head, and still held him with a steady look.

'Maybe I'll find out, if I look around myself,' I said. 'How about it? No more than ten minutes. If I get the answer, I'll come down to the desk and tell you about it. And maybe a brother to one of those tens, too. A deal?'

He stared at me intently out of greedy eyes. Then, suddenly, he did a strange thing for a bird like him. He smiled and shook his head.

'No dough, mister,' he said. 'You've been a right enough guy. So go ahead and take your time. Nobody else on this floor, anyway. So you don't need to bother about some bozo sticking his head in.'

With a nod, a wink, and a wave of his hand, he turned and went out of the room, softly closing the door behind him. I didn't move for a minute, maybe two. Then I took a quick step to the door, and yanked it open and stuck my head out. The result was that the Barnes felt a little foolish, and a little sore at himself. I mean, the little bald-headed guy wasn't there with an eye to the keyhole. He wasn't even in the hallway. Nobody was. I stepped back into the room and closed the door.

The problem was where to start, because nothing seemed to be in one piece. Everything, big and small, was scattered here and there. I decided to begin with a small, flat, well-worn leather case that was half hidden under the corner of a dirty pillow slip at my feet. I reached down, picked it up, undid the flap snap, and took a look. I had struck paydirt first try. It was as neat a set of burglar tools as I've ever seen.

As I stared at it I wondered if it had been part of Cardeur's standard underground equipment, or whether he had used it by way of picking up a little 'business' on the side. Then when I poked a finger in the flap pocket, I brought something else of interest into the poor light of the room. It was a bead chain, and hanging on the chain were at least fifteen keys of all shapes and sizes. A couple of them were even blanks. Not being that kind of an expert, I wasn't able to say for sure. But I was willing to bet quite a sum that that collection of keys would open an awful lot of locks, both plain and fancy. And because I was willing to make that bet, I slipped the ring of keys into my pocket and tossed the case of burglar tools back onto the floor.

Twenty minutes later, I got up from my hands and knees, brushed half a peck of feathers from my clothes, and mopped my sweat-beaded face with my handkerchief. I had done the room, to coin a phrase, but hadn't come up with a single thing. Not a single thing that had so much as caused me to take a second look. Maurice Cardeur, if that was his real name, certainly traveled light, and with a minimum of personal effects. A stranger searching the place wouldn't have even found out what his name was. As far as I could see, there wasn't a single piece of paper with writing or printing on it.

And then, suddenly, as I brushed off the last clinging pillow feather, I saw that I was wrong. At the bottom of an overturned waste-paper basket was a crumpled sheet of paper. Plain paper, perhaps, but I stepped over, bent down and pulled it out just in case not. And it was not just plain paper. Just one side was plain. The other side was completely covered with at least fifty signatures. But the signatures were all the same name.

And the name was . . . Herbert Varney.

That, of course, didn't mean a thing to me. For a couple of moments. And then when I'd stopped wondering, and took a good look, I saw the signatures at the bottom of the sheet were slightly different from those at the top. And from there I went on to note that there was actually a gradual difference in the way the name was signed right from the top down to the bottom. In short, undoubtedly the original signature of somebody named Herbert Varney had been copied and copied until all the little characteristic scrawls and flourishes were as they should be.

'So?' I echoed my thoughts aloud. 'Maurice Cardeur, safe cracking, lock picking, and forgery at reasonable rates?'

The sound of my very unfunny voice startled me. I quickly shoved the sheet of signatures into my pocket, as though I was afraid somebody was watching, and called an end to my search. I went out, and down the hall, and down the two flights to the desk. The little baldheaded guy was all eyes and ears as I walked up.

'You musta found something, taking

that long, huh?' he asked expectantly.

I shook my head, and looked disappointed-sore.

'Not a thing,' I grunted. 'I wasted my time. Here.'

As I started to slide a ten across the desk, he shook his bald head violently and raised a protesting hand.

'Forget it, mister,' he said. 'I know a right gent when I see one, see?'

'No, you take it,' I said, and left the bill where I'd pushed it. 'For something extra. To forget you ever saw me. Maybe some more of his pals will be dropping by. I don't want any of them to know I was there. Get it?'

He shook his head, and I set myself for the well-known hold-up. However, it seemed to be the Barnes day for guessing wrong.

'I don't get it, mister,' he said with a grin. 'But that's okay. Lots of things goes on in this dump that I don't get. But don't worry none. I never seen you in my life before. And thanks, mister.'

I waved at him not to give it a thought and went down the angling stairs to the street. On the sidewalk I paused for a few moments to light a cigarette, but the big idea was to take a really good look in all directions. A familiar feeling was crawling up the back of my neck. It was a feeling that had come to me more than a few times in the war. Usually it had worked out that there was a sniper nearby, or a passing patrol. In other words, a premonition of danger right close at hand.

This time, though, the old warning didn't mean a thing. At least as far as I could see. Nobody was hiding behind a lamp post or anything. Nor was there any car with drawn shades whispering softly down the street. However, to check I turned and walked casually toward Broadway, stopping every now and then for a look into store windows. No soap. Only my screwy imagination was tagging along after me.

At Broadway I flagged a cab and drove to the building where my office is located. The bootblack and the cigar-counter lad gave mc a grin and an interested lift of the eyebrows. They, of course, had read all about DeFoe in yesterday's papers. Something, by the way, which I had not.

So I simply grinned at both of them, bought myself three late editions, and took the elevator up.

I was in luck, you might say. Nobody, not even a reporter, was parked with his lunch box outside my office door. Frankly, I had half expected a cop, but there was no lad in blue. My key worked the lock, too. I stepped into my office, closed the door, and took a good look around. I silently tipped my hat to Bierman, and thanked him very much. The office was exactly as I had left it some twenty-eight hours before. Of course DeFoe, and all reminders of him, had been removed. But not another single thing, as far as I could notice. Bierman certainly respected other people's property. Even when said people were inclined to rub him the wrong way. Hardly believing it, I went around in back of my desk and pulled open the left lower drawer. And there was final proof, if I needed it. I mean, the rye bottle was still there, and its liquid contents at the same level.

I regarded it gravely, decided no, and

sat down at my desk. I took the chain of keys, and the sheet of signatures from my pocket, and spent several thoughtful moments over them. Presently I got up and went over to my office door. When I went back and sat down again, a very important piece of the screwy jigsaw puzzle had fitted into its correct place.

I did some thinking about this and that, and then came up with an idea. I had lost Parrish's address and phone number, along with his five hundred dollars, but fortunately I could remember them. So I pulled over the phone and dialed the number. The sound of his bell-buzz came over the wire three times, and then the receiver was lifted at his end.

'Yes?'

Just the sound of a single word, but to me it was like stepping on a live wire. In case it was simply my imagination making a flat turn, I made sure. I dropped my voice a little and slurred it some.

'Mr. Gordon Parrish?' I asked politely.

'No. Who's calling, please?'

Then I knew, and knowing somehow made my day all sunny and bright. The voice that spoke to me had been thin and reedy. For the second time I had heard it, and not been able to see its owner!

'A friend,' I said quickly. 'Let me speak to him. It's important!'

There was a moment's hesitation, and I set myself for an argument with Reedy Voice. No need for it, though.

'Just a minute, please,' Reedy Voice told me. 'Hold on.'

I held on for about two seconds flat, and then Parrish's voice came on the wire.

'Gordon Parrish speaking,' he said, very business-like. 'Who is this?'

I sat perfectly still, so that I wouldn't miss a thing. I even closed my eyes, the better to concentrate, or something.

'This is Barnes, Parrish,' I said quietly.

Check! And double check. I heard the quick intake of breath, as though he were sitting in my lap.

'What? *Who?*' Maybe he had tried hard to make it casual. But it still sounded more like a couple of rifle shots.

'Barnes,' I repeated. 'Gerry Barnes. You hired me for a little job. Remember?'

'Oh, Barnes?' he echoed right up the scale. Then hurriedly, 'Yes, yes, of course. Where are you?'

'In my office,' I replied. And I would have given a very big chunk of dough to be looking at his face. 'I want to see you,' I added. 'Soon as possible. Got a few things to report. You want to come here, or do you want me to drop over to your place?'

I gave it to him that way with a purpose. I wanted to see what kind of a choice he'd make. I had a hunch that his choice would tell me a couple of other things. He took roughly twenty seconds to make his choice.

'I . . . I think it would be better for you to come here, Mr. Barnes,' he finally told me. 'And come right away, will you? I have another appointment, but I'll put it off.'

'Five minutes,' I said with a grin he couldn't see. 'Don't go away.'

He assured me that he wouldn't, and hung up. I hung up and leaned back, still grinning. Pensively I lifted a hand to my head that still had an ache here and there, and a couple of lumps that had not quite flattened down to normal.

'So Parrish got scared?' I murmured to myself aloud. 'Yeah. The guy got scared as hell!'

And by way of emphasis for that, my phone bell rang. I didn't pick it up. I was afraid it was Parrish calling off the meeting. At least postponing it. And I definitely wanted to see that lad, and Reedy Voice, very soon and quick. So I let the thing ring a couple of times before my curiosity won. It wasn't Gordon Parrish.

It was Lieutenant Bierman.

'That you, Barnes?' he barked.

''Tis me,' I replied. 'What do you want?'

'I want to see you right away, Barnes,' he said. 'Meet me at . . . '

'Sorry, Lieutenant,' I cut in. 'I have a very important appointment that won't keep. Maybe — '

'It will have to keep!' he broke in on me. 'I don't care what kind of an appointment it is. Mine's more important. Do I make myself clear?'

I was tempted to hang up on him, but

common sense stopped such foolishness. When Bierman talked like that, he wasn't kidding. And I didn't want to have him gunning for my license . . . yet.

'Okay, okay,' I grunted. 'Meet you in your office?'

'No,' he said. 'Not in my office. Meet me at the Bellevue Morgue, Barnes.'

Half of my stomach dropped a couple of inches. The other half became frozen solid. 'At the what?' I automatically gasped.

'The *Morgue!*' he snapped. 'You hear me, Barnes? The Bellevue Morgue!'

'Yes, sure,' I said with an effort. 'The Bellevue Morgue. Coming, now.'

The line clicked, and went dead.

14

When I climbed out of my taxi, Bierman was waiting for me. And so was the ·ever-present Sergeant Goff. I went over to them quickly, a dozen questions battling to get off my tongue first.

'What gives?' was what I finally demanded.

Bierman shrugged and started up the steps.

'I'd like to know that very much,' he said bluntly. Then, with a side glance I couldn't miss, or misconstrue either, he added, 'I'm hoping you can tell me.'

If there was comment from me expected, it did not materialize. I had several funny little feelings batting around inside of me, and worry was definitely one of them. Why worry — ? I didn't know, but I was certainly worried as we three went inside. The lad in charge knew Bierman and Goff of course, and nodded a greeting. The pale, vacant eyes he brushed over me made me shiver.

'The same guy, Lieutenant?' he asked Bierman.

Bierman nodded, and we all moved along the chilly room. The lad in charge stopped in front of one of those cabinet combinations, and then pulled out the slab. What was on the slab was covered by a sheet. Of course I was nuts, but it seemed to me the guy was living one of the high spots of his day. The way he seemed to pause with one top corner of the sheet in his hand, and then look us all over one by one. Very un-theatrical for my money. I wanted to bark at him to cut it out.

Then he pulled back the sheet.

If you've ever seen a dead man who has been in the water for a while, then you know exactly what I looked at when I took a look. Death I've seen a couple of thousand times or more, but each new time is a mule kick to the belly for me. This time was no exception.

However, it didn't last so long because I knew that three pairs of eyes, two pairs anyway, were watching me like hawks. I had steeled myself for almost anything, and was glad I had. I didn't meet anybody's gaze. I held my eyes on the stiff, it seemed like for a hundred years.

'Well?'

Bierman's single word rocked around that stone cavern like a roll of thunder. I forced myself to look up and at him.

'Well?' I said right back, calmly, I hoped.

'Stop it!' he snapped. 'I never play games in this place. You know him, don't you?'

I looked in his eyes and debated it. But not for long. A very wise little voice inside of me warned me not to try and pick all the apples for myself. Sharing a few might keep me out of trouble longer. I nodded.

'Yes,' I said. 'His name's Maurice Cardeur. What's the story, anyway?'

My unexpected truthful answer caught Bierman off guard. He had been all prepared to cloud up and thunderstorm all over me.

'A police boat fished him out of the Hudson, off Ninety-Sixth,' he said. 'Early this morning.'

'Yes?' I murmured, and waited.

He guessed what I was thinking in back of that, and gave a little shrug.

'The routine check by us got my interest,' he said. He started to say more, but suddenly seemed to think that covered it. It didn't, for me.

'You said you didn't play games in here, and neither do I,' I said. 'I could have bluffed a lie, but I didn't. Why did the routine check get *your* interest, Lieutenant?'

'He was dead before he was dumped in the river,' he said, as though reciting something from memory. Then, pointing, 'That lump on his head he got either before or after he was scragged. The doc thinks before. Split seconds before.'

My jaw had dropped, so I lifted it up and swallowed hard. 'Scragged?' I echoed. 'You mean . . . ?'

'I do, yes,' he stepped on the rest of my question. 'Garroted by fine steel wire. Right off the same piece that finished DeFoe. Two of the crimped-off ends matched. That's why I had the hunch you could tell us who he was.'

'No identification on him, huh?' I murmured the question impulsively.

He shook his head, and gave me a funny twisted grin. 'Not a thing. He'd been cleaned as clean as you were cleaned, Barnes.'

I didn't miss what he meant, but I ignored it. At least for the time being. I was too busy thinking of other things. To have the little runt, Maurice Cardeur, come up dead like this knocked several of my jigsaw puzzle pieces onto the floor. Instead of feeling sorry for the little guy, I was sore at him for having messed up the parade but good.

'What are you thinking, Barnes?' Bierman's voice broke into my thoughts. 'Certainly removes the number-one suspect, doesn't it?'

I just shrugged. 'Need we hold this wake any longer?' I demanded. 'I could do with some fresh air. Even the un-fresh air you've got down at Centre Street.'

'How was that?' he asked with a sharp look.

I was already turning away from the slab, and what was on it. 'Your office, if you're not busy,' I said over my shoulder. 'Maybe at this point it'd help if we had a little talk. If you're not too busy?'

I saw the start of a grin that went racing across his lips just before I turned my head front. 'Too busy?' he echoed. 'Not at all, Barnes. Not at all. I'm never too busy to talk things over with you.'

I let that ride without comment. I would need all of the ten minutes it would take us to make Centre Street Police Headquarters to do a lot of heavy, fast, and furious thinking. And I used up every one of the nine minutes it actually was, even though Bierman tried half a dozen times to start a conversation. When we were finally in his office he tried again, and made the grade because I was all through thinking by then.

'One thing before we start, Barnes,' he said, fixing his eyes on me from across the desk. 'If this is just a fishing trip for you, forget it. I don't know one tenth of what you know about this thing. And I'm certainly not telling you what little I do know. Okay, go ahead.'

'Wrong, Bierman, wrong,' I said sadly,

and smiled that way, too. 'Frankly, what we both know doesn't even add up to one tenth. Anyway, it seems like that to me. Who do you think scragged DeFoe and Cardeur?'

'Who do you think?' he shot right back.

'See what I mean?' I said. 'The truth is, we both know damn close to from nothing.'

'I'd like to have a Bible here,' he presently said flatly, 'and make you put your hand on it.'

'And I would, I definitely would,' I told him brightly. Then, getting really serious, 'There is one thing I would like, though, Lieutenant.'

'I thought so!' he barked. 'And the answer is no!'

'Okay, okay,' I soothed him. 'Then I'll just have to find out some other way. I hope.'

He didn't like that at all, of course.

He wanted so much to give me the vocal works, and maybe a couple of other things. But he was too smart for that. Incidentally, that was one of the several reasons he was tops in his profession, and held the top-drawer job he held. But he had to take a moment or two to simmer down.

'All right, all right,' he growled. 'We're both just wasting time with this kind of chit-chat. I know damn well you know more than we do, if for no other reason than that you're in a position to know more. However, the big thing is to break these two killings. If you can do it before we do, at least the job will be done. Okay, what is it you want? And when you tell me, I'm going to ask why.'

His little speech had been straight, without a single curve. I liked him for that. In fact, I suddenly liked him so much that I was tempted to reveal a couple of items that he and the boys definitely didn't know. However, I decided not to.

'Have you still got the stuff you took off DeFoe?' I asked.

'Certainly we have,' he came right back. 'And I'm asking it. Why?'

'I'd like to look it over,' I said casually.

'I'm still asking it,' he told me. 'Why?'

I leaned forward to crush out the three quarters of an inch of my cigarette in one of his desk trays. 'This is the truth,' I said solemnly. 'I don't know, exactly. I simply have a hunch . . . a damn strong one . . . that you've missed something.'

A little wry smile tugged at the corners of his mouth. 'It wouldn't be the first time,' he said bluntly. 'Or probably the last. But just what is your hunch?'

'Just a hunch,' I said, 'that . . . ' I stopped myself cold as a thought came to me.

'Yes?' Bierman grunted. 'Now what?'

'A thought,' I admitted. 'Should have asked you before. When you went through his pockets, did it strike you that somebody else had been through them . . . ?'

'Maybe you aren't just a playboy in this racket, Barnes,' he chuckled. 'When you don't know something, you make a guess. Usually it's a good one.'

'Like this time, huh?' I grinned.

'Like this time.' He nodded. 'DeFoe had been searched. It was simple enough to see that. A couple of things were in pockets where a man wouldn't usually carry them. So maybe there goes your hunch, eh? What you hoped to find, the killer found. Right?'

Definitely Bierman was right. What's more, I was beginning to get just a hazy idea of what it had been that DeFoe's killer took away with him. Anyway, I hoped it was the beginning of an idea. However, I didn't let Bierman know I thought he was right. And I certainly didn't mention anything about my growing an idea. I simply shrugged.

'Could be yes, and could be no,' I said. 'So I'd still like to take a look at the stuff. And you can watch me look at it, of course.'

He didn't answer. He put out a hand and flipped up the switch of his inter-office com-box. 'Bring in the stuff found on that Frenchman, DeFoe,' he told somebody at the other end.

'Thanks.' I grinned when he snapped off and leaned back in his chair. Then, while we both waited, I added, 'By the way, any report on the time Cardeur slid out of it all?'

Bierman nodded. 'About nine o'clock last night,' he said. Then, with just the ghost of a grin, 'At that time you were where?'

I took it for the rib it was and grinned back at him. 'Bull's eye!' I said. 'And don't I wish I knew!'

'You really don't, Barnes?' he asked slowly.

'I really don't,' I said firmly. And with plenty of grimness. 'But I figure to find out, among other things.'

'Ideas and plans, huh?' he murmured.

I was shaking my head vigorously when his office door opened and one of the Centre Street boys came in with the stuff taken out of DeFoe's pockets. It was in a big manila envelope. He put it on the desk and went away. Bierman opened the envelope and dumped its contents on his blotter.

'Go ahead and look,' he said. 'I'll even let you sit down in my chair.'

To prove it, he got up and walked over to the double windows. I got up and walked around his desk, and sat down in his chair. I knew that he was watching my every move, and particularly the expressions that came and went on my face, if any. I didn't care much, though. He'd had first crack at the stuff, and if he couldn't get anything out of it then that was his tough luck. I picked up DeFoe's wallet and breathed a little prayer that *I* wouldn't have tough luck.

Ten minutes later I pushed the stuff away, blew an exasperated sigh through my lips, and sat back. Bierman walked over from the window.

'And so?' he grunted.

'Nothing,' I lied. Then, with a little wave of one hand at the pile of stuff, 'Did you look up any of the addresses in that little black book?' I asked casually.

'The New York ones.' He nodded. 'All importing firms. Perfumes, jewelry, cosmetics, and stuff like that. Small firms. Huh! Even when I only see DeFoe scragged, I can still picture him dealing in that sort of junk. Quite a guy with the ladies, no doubt. Slick-looking smoothies like that always seem to get them. I wonder why.'

'You and the rest of our male population,' I grunted, and got to my feet. 'Well, thanks, Lieutenant. I now know exactly no more than I did!'

He looked at me, half smiling, but his

eyes slitted. 'That's tough,' he murmured. 'I was rather hoping, Barnes.'

I put on my hat, and grinned right back at him. 'Well, I identified Cardeur for you,' I said. 'I guess you'll have to call that my good deed for the day.'

'I guess I'll have to,' he murmured, and turned to face the window again. 'Well, be seeing you, Barnes. Drop in any time.'

As I walked out of his office, I wondered if he had flashed any signal out the window to somebody down below, maybe in another office. However, I didn't wonder very much. I was too busy memorizing over and over a few of the addresses I had seen in DeFoe's little black book.

15

The place where Gordon Parrish lived was in the West Fifties, just over from the corner of Eighth Avenue. And when my taxi pulled up in front of it, I was somehow surprised to see that it was a fairly modern building. A six-story apartment-house affair that gave you the impression it was glancing down askance at the familiar brown-stone rooming houses that flanked both sides, and even faced it on the other side of the street.

In the small entrance lobby, the two rows of name cards told me that Parrish was in Five-C. I looked at the other names to see if there were any I should know, but there weren't. A punch-button elevator took me up and let me out at five. Five-C was at the front, at the end of the short hallway. I wondered if Parrish had watched my taxi pull up and seen me get out. As a matter of fact, I wondered quite a few things as I made that short walk. At the end of it, I checked to see that my holstered gun was the way I like it, and then put my thumb on the bell button.

The door was pulled open split seconds later, and there stood the tall, thin guy I thought I had lost in Radio City. He smiled as though I was one person he was very glad to see.

'Mr. Barnes?' he wanted to know.

Well, so that was that, and at long last. Thin face and Reedy Voice were one and the same person! That pleased me, if only that it cut down the field by one. I smiled right back at him.

'Yes, and I was held up. Sorry,' I said. 'Mr. Parrish waited, I hope?'

'Oh, yes, yes!' He beamed, and swung the door wide and stood back. 'Come in, please.'

I went in, but my skin did crawl a little as I walked by him. Maybe I just don't like tall, thin lads with that kind of a voice to be so happy when they see me. Anyway, he didn't do anything about it. He closed the door, snapped the bolt lock, and then guided me through a five-foot hallway, or foyer I guess, and into the apartment living room. I saw that it was slightly small, that it had some furniture, and then I saw Parrish. He was at a wall desk, writing maybe, but he had stopped and half turned around. When he saw me, he got up and came over to shake hands.

'I was afraid that you'd suddenly forgotten, Mr. Barnes,' he said. 'Here, try this chair. A cigarette, sir? A drink, perhaps?'

I shook my head twice and dropped into the chair. 'A little matter on another case popped up,' I said, and casually hitched my chair a little so that they both had to sit down more or less in front of me. 'Couldn't put it off, and I didn't think it would take more than a minute. Sorry that it did.'

Parrish's gesture was quite magnanimous. 'Quite all right, sir,' he said. 'Franz and I had no place to go, and . . . Oh, I beg your pardon, sir. And yours, Franz. Mr. Barnes, I would like you to meet Franz Eurlich. Franz, this, as you know, is Mr. Barnes, whom I hired to find

Maurice for me.'

I didn't like the 'hired' and I didn't like the 'for me.' In fact, I didn't like any part of it. However, I went through the act of shaking hands with Eurlich, and smiling warmly. And I looked into his face but good, and wondered if he had so much as an inkling of my yearning to knock his fang-like teeth all the way down his throat. Truth to tell, I would have given a pretty penny to know just what he was thinking at the moment. He didn't tell me, though, and when the cordial act was completed, Parrish got right down to cases.

'You said over the phone you had a few things to report, sir?' he murmured. 'Good news, I hope? You've found Maurice Cardeur for me? Where the devil has he been all this time?'

It was the dramatic in me, I guess. And the corn, too. I mean, I didn't reply at once. I waited while they both leaned forward, eyes clamped on me.

'In the Hudson River,' I said quietly.

When the echo of my words died away, you could have heard a feather crash against another feather. Eurlich suddenly broke it with a questioning curse in a tongue I didn't catch. Parrish stared at me blank-eyed a moment longer.

'Did you say in the Hudson River?' he asked like a punch-drunk boxer asking his seconds what round it was.

'That's right,' I told him, 'A police boat fished him out very early this morning. Ten minutes ago I saw him in the Bellevue Morgue. He was not nice to see.'

Again the very silent silence. It was not the reaction I had expected. It was not even close. I had the crazy feeling that I was on a treadmill. A thought treadmill, you might call it. My partially worked-out jigsaw puzzle seemed to be kicked into a heap of jumbled pieces.

'That is a lie! That is not so! You lie!'

The words came out in a gurgled scream. I was more than flabbergasted for maybe the millionth part of a second. Just long enough to realize that the words had come from Eurlich, and to see him lunging at me with his thin claw-like fingers aimed for my neck. Well, I always like to protect myself. Also, this was as good a time as later. So I let him come. Almost to his goal. Then I swayed away and came up on my feet. My right fist came up, too. It connected dead center under his outthrust jaw. To make it complete, I had hooked my left foot behind his right, just touching the floor. You get one hundred percent leverage that way, if you know just how to do it. The OSS had made sure that I did!

The top half of Eurlich went snapping back, and the bottom half of him came snapping forward. He turned a complete loop and landed on his face and belly. Landed, and stayed right there. The thought occurred to me that maybe I had snapped his scrawny neck. I really didn't care, yes or no. I was still on my feet and looking straight at Parrish. He looked like he was sitting in a bucket of tar that had hardened. Not a muscle moving. Not even his eyes. They were fixed by invisible steel rods to his long, skinny friend on the floor.

'Your friend must be nuts, Parrish,' I said. Then, as mounting anger choked in my throat, 'What the hell was he trying, anyway?'

It looked like it took every bit of Parrish's strength for him to take his eyes off Eurlich and look at me. It was almost a full minute before he spoke.

'Franz must be mad to think that you . . . I mean . . . '

He was so tangled up he had to stop. I stared at him. And believe it or not, I suddenly wondered if I was looking at a lad who could have been one of the finest actors in the world, if he'd wanted to. I waited for him to go on, because I'd had my say.

'My most sincere apologies, Mr. Barnes,' he suddenly blurted out. 'Please, I beg you to forgive Franz. You see, Maurice was his dearest friend. Three times Maurice saved Franz's life in the war. To think Maurice was dead was a shock. You understand? Grief can make men do such strange things.'

Very good, and maybe he meant it, too. But my neck was still tingling from fingers that hadn't quite reached it. I glanced down at the thin guy. He was right where I had planted him. If I knew my right uppercuts, he would be listening to the birdies for quite a spell. I looked at Parrish again. He was still sad, and bewildered, and humbly apologetic. But there was something else in his ugly face, too. Something I wasn't quite able to give a name to.

'Whatever he thought, it's still as is,' I said. 'Cardeur is dead. You read yesterday's papers, of course?'

He started slightly, and a lot of that sadness and humble apology started to go away. 'DeFoe?' he murmured. 'Yes. I have been thinking, Mr. Barnes. It had happened when I met you outside your office building, yes?'

'Yes.' I nodded.

He mulled it over with a frown. He stared down at his hands, one on each knee, and then up at me under slightly lowered brows.

'You knew, but you did not tell me,' he said.

'No, I didn't,' I said evenly. 'But you didn't hire me to find DeFoe. You hired me to find Cardeur. Which I have.'

He nodded faintly, and then stared some more down at his hands on his knees. Maybe he was going over this and that, or maybe he was stalling for time. I didn't care which. I had a couple of more arrows in my quiver.

'You don't seem interested enough to ask, Parrish,' I said. 'Or do you know?'

He looked up quickly, and I knew he hadn't caught my true meaning.

'The way Cardeur died,' I said, and watched him.

'Why . . . why, from drowning, wasn't it?' he echoed. 'At least that's what I gather.'

'You gather wrong,' I told him bluntly. 'He was garroted. Like DeFoe. The police are very annoyed. So am I, for that matter. I do not like to be paid off for dead men.'

That last he did get. Maybe because it had taken up a lot of his thoughts since the moment I reported that I had found Cardeur. Anyway, he slowly reached into his inside jacket pocket, and pulled out his wallet. He counted out a thousand in fifties and hundreds, and held the lot out to me. I took it. I took it and looked at it, and wondered. I mean, if I was holding in my hand the thousand bucks that Henri Barone had given me in Goldilocks' apartment yesterday noon, I wished with all that was in me that I could prove it. I sighed and put the money in my pocket.

All the time, Parrish was watching me and saying nothing. What a wonderful detective I would be if I could only read minds. I was willing to bet anything that the last thing in the world Parrish was thinking about was the money he had just handed over. Anyway, I decided that there was nothing more to be gained by hanging around. Also, I had other things to do, and as soon as I could. I picked up my hat off the arm of my chair and stuck it on my head.

'Well, get in touch with the Bellevue Morgue if you want to claim Cardeur's body, Parrish,' I said. 'But it'll probably be a spell before they'll release it. He was murdered, you know.'

He nodded his head slowly twice, and said nothing. He was definitely Rodin's *Thinker* in street clothes. I looked down at Eurlich and saw that he was breathing normally. So I hadn't snapped his damn

181

neck. Too bad. I started to turn toward the door, then glanced back at Parrish.

'Give your friend the drink you offered me,' I said. 'And a word of advice for him, too, when he's finished it. I do not like people to shadow me around. Definitely, I do not like tall thin characters. Be sure and tell him that. *Adieu*, Parrish.'

I went out of there feeling quite the boy. But as I rode down in the punch-button elevator, the feeling went away. One of being very foolish took its place. I was worried about just how *much* my big mouth had conveyed to Gordon Parrish!

16

From a drugstore on Eighth, I tried Paula's apartment again, but it was still no soap. A tiny quiver of worry went through me, but it kept right on going away. Paula definitely wasn't a stay-at-home. Besides, later, around the cocktail hour, I should be able to find her.

So I put the lovely gorgeous redheaded gal from my mind, and phoned her direct opposite, at least in my book. Goldilocks was home, and when she learned who was at the other end, she practically came swimming down the wire. Yes, yes, she wasn't going out. Certainly not now. And it was so nice to hear my voice. And, please, sweet Gerry, come up at once. Mush, gush, and slush, but I finally managed to turn it off.

'Look, beautiful, can you get in touch with Parkus and Barone?' I wanted to know.

Full stop, with silence, too. 'Why,

Gerry? I want so much to see you most. I — '

'Mutual,' I cut in to be gallant. 'But I want to see them right away. After all, I'm working for Barone, you know. I've got a thing or two to tell him.'

'A thing or two, Gerry, darling?' Slowly. 'What thing or two, eh?'

'You'll hear it when I tell them,' I said. 'Can you get hold of them? Pretty please, baby. The Barnes will make it up . . . you know?'

There was so much silence I thought for a moment that we had been cut off. We hadn't. The little slick chick was taking a leaf from Parrish's book, no doubt. Thinking hard. And furiously, no?

'Very well, Gerry,' she finally pouted over the Bell System. 'I will call Henri at once. But you come at once, eh? I have been worried about you. Not since yesterday I have heard. I call your apartment, but you are not there. And that beautiful Miss Grant! If she knows something, she will not tell it to me. But I do not worry now. You are close.'

'And I'll get closer,' I said gravely. 'Be

seeing you, Goldilocks.'

I hung up, went outside and started to flag a cab, but checked myself. I decided to give her time to get in touch with Parkus and Barone. And also to give them time to get there before I did. For a couple of reasons. One of them being that I wasn't up to wrestling and fighting for my good name today! So I went into the nearest pub and dilly-dallied over a couple of Scotches that weren't half bad, considering the location in town. After that I did flag a cab and gave the driver Zara's address.

My dilly-dallying in the pub paid off as I had hoped it would. When Zara Zaralis opened the apartment door at my ring, I had only to look past her to see Barone and Parkus all set with a drink apiece. Goldilocks' greeting was mostly with her hands, and the smile on her face. Which the other two could not see. To me she looked pretty okay, considering that last night she had stepped a few fast rounds with an unknown intruder. There was just the bare traces of a couple of scratches on her face, the left side. Cream, powder, and such had been put to work with a fine art, believe me.

Both Barone and Parkus were on their feet when we reached the sort of sunken living room. Parkus still had his grin, but there didn't seem to be much of it in his eyes this meeting. He widened his grin a little, and gave me a silent salute with his drink. I gave him the same kind right back, minus the drink.

Henri Barone seemed to look dirtier than ever. But maybe that was because he had his brows pulled well down, and was regarding me with a mixture of anxiety and impatience. He nodded, murmured a greeting, and sat down again, still looking at me. I just let him look while I selected a chair that would only hold one. I sat down and made like I didn't see Zara's pout as she settled herself kitten-style on the divan. Then I popped it on the three of them. Right, smack, quick out of the box.

'I've found Maurice Cardeur.'

It is hard to look at three faces at the same time. But I did my best, and got results that didn't boost my spirits a terrible lot. The three of them leaned forward quickly, mouths opening. Barone won.

'You have? Where?'

'In the Bellevue Morgue,' I said.

Andy Parkus' fixed smile went out just like Barone's face seemed to drop two inches, and freeze. Goldilocks sucked in air, and half reached out a trembling hand.

'In the . . . the what, Gerry?' she gasped.

'The Bellevue Morgue,' I repeated. Then, in case they didn't know, I explained, 'That's where they take people found dead. And keep them there for identification, and claiming by the next of kin, if there is one. He was pulled out of the Hudson River early this morning. He'd been garroted. The same way, as of course you know now, that René DeFoe was murdered. It was I who identified Cardeur for the police.'

There it was, just about all of it. I leaned back to look, and to wait. What I saw was Barone and Parkus take their eyes off me and look at Goldilocks. They looked at her, and frowned a little. But she didn't cringe, or anything like. *If* anything like that was expected. She sat with her hand still half outstretched toward me. Her face was a stunned blank, and her eyes the color of a cheap brand of bluing. Suddenly she shook her head violently, clenched her hands into two little fists, and pressed them together up in front of her chin.

'It cannot be murder!' she cried. 'It cannot. Suicide, perhaps, yes. Maurice could be like that. How many the times have I heard him declare so. But murder. No, no, *no*!'

'Yes,' I said quietly. 'I saw the body. It was Cardeur's.'

'You were mistaken, Zara,' Barone suddenly spoke, in a voice that sounded lifeless. 'Could it not be that you were mistaken? That Maurice did not come here to be the jealous fool?'

Of course it clicked with me at once what he was talking about. But I kept my face blank to give the impression it was all going over my head. I could feel Parkus suddenly watching me closely, but I was too busy watching the Zaralis chick. Her face was flaming now, and there were real tears in her eyes.

'But it was Maurice!' she cried. Then, thrusting them out, 'Do I not have hands that can feel? I tell you I felt his face as we struggled. It was Maurice's face. It . . . I do not understand! This is . . . is all of the madness!'

'Why did you lie to Lieutenant Bierman?'

Yes, it was the Barnes voice. Cracking like a whip. And she reacted like the end had caught her right across her pretty mouth . . . that was all twisted and not at all pretty at the moment.

'Lieutenant Bierman?' she got out weakly. 'Then you know?'

'I know,' I said, and there was none of the beauty-smitten dead duck in my voice, or in my eyes. 'He told me that you didn't know whether it was a man or a woman.'

'I . . . I . . . ' She stopped there, and choked up. 'I could not tell *him*!' she finally made it. 'He would punish my Maurice!'

And when that was out, she put her two hands to her face and cried with great shaking sobs that came all the way up from her toes. If the other two had not been there, I might have tried to do something about soothing her. But I decided it was better to just look my sympathy.

'*Monsieur* Barnes, what you have told us is a great shock,' Barone said in a dull, dead voice. 'But for Zara . . . it is enough to crush the heart. You see *monsieur* . . . ?'

He paused and looked at me out of tragic eyes.

'They were everything to each other,' he said at length. 'It began in France when they met. *Monsieur* Barnes, it was not so much for myself as for Zara, I wished you to find Maurice. You understand? You see?'

I wasn't particularly touched. If I had been, I might have been just a little less brutally blunt. 'Not quite,' I said. 'Lieutenant Bierman told me something else. That this apartment is . . . was . . . in René DeFoe's name.'

If I had expected Barone to look shocked, and Goldilocks to redden to the roots of her hair, I was completely out of luck. She went right on weeping, but with less noise. And Barone simply looked at me as though I'd told him Lincoln was shot.

'But what of that, *monsieur*?' he murmured. 'In this country that is no crime.'

'Definitely not.' I tried to get back some of my edge. 'And in your country it is quite the usual thing.'

'Most certainly,' he said. Then as though the thought had hit him hard, he asked quickly, 'Do you mean that Lieutenant Bierman suspects Zara of that swine's death?'

'DeFoe's?' I said to make sure.

'Who else?' he came back sharply. 'Certainly DeFoe, *monsieur*! And it would be absurd to think any such thing of Zara! Why should she murder DeFoe?'

'I wouldn't know,' I said. 'Tell me, Barone, when did you learn about DeFoe's end?'

At that point the ex-GI, Andy Parkus,

broke into the conversation. 'Five minutes after we left you yesterday, Barnes,' he said. 'The newspapers had just hit the street. Why didn't you tell us?'

I looked at him and grinned. 'Nobody asked me a thing about DeFoe,' I said. 'It was all about Cardeur. But now that we've brought DeFoe up, have you any idea who killed him?'

He nodded, and my heart leaped a little.

'A couple of dozen ideas, Barnes,' he said with that damned grin. 'All guys who hated his guts. Me being one of them. What do you think of that?'

'That you certainly didn't,' I told him evenly. 'Garroting is not the American style.'

'My mother was Swiss-French.' He grinned.

'It still stays as is,' I said, and turned my attention to Barone. 'What are your ideas?'

He seemed not to hear at first. His eyes that were fixed on space told me one of two things: he was either really knocked for a loop by the news of Cardeur's death, or else he was doing a whole lot of concentrated thinking. I could take my choice. Before I could, he snapped out of it and looked at me.

'I do not know enough for ideas yet, *monsieur*,' he said slowly. 'Perhaps if you would tell me why he came to see you at your office, I would then know something?'

I opened my mouth, then shut it, and wagged my head. 'Sorry,' I said. 'I never divulge a client's secrets. Neither before or after his murder. But what about Cardeur? They obviously hated each other's insides, but of course DeFoe didn't kill Cardeur. DeFoe was already dead.'

Barone started to speak, but a funny hissing gasp from Zara Zaralis stopped him. We all looked at her, and she wasn't a pathetic, sobbing, cute little trick now. She was a seething bundle of boiling-over TNT.

'Zara!' Barone said sharply.

She shivered, blinked, and looked at him out of rage-glazed eyes. 'That one!' she fairly spat out. 'No other. *Parrish*!'

Andy Parkus jerked up in his chair next

to mine. 'Jesus!' he said in a hoarse whisper. 'Could be!'

I looked at Barone, and waited. He was certainly a guy of moods. Or maybe that face of his gave you the impression of rapidly changing moods. This time he seemed to be grinning inwardly. He swiveled his eyes around to mine.

'Did you kill Maurice, *monsieur?*' he asked.

Me kill the guy? I was so jolted by that totally unexpected bit that I couldn't find my tongue for a moment, or slap the cover back on my zooming temper.

'Where the hell do you get that stuff?' I blazed.

He looked at my head and face for a moment, and then slowly moved his gaze down to the part of my jacket that covered my holstered gun.

'You have been in a fight, *monsieur,*' he said quietly. 'A very hard fight, perhaps. And today you are carrying a gun. Should one not consider the possibility a little, eh?'

'Not even a little,' I told him flat out. Then, flicking a hand at my head, I told him, 'I got these lumps in the line of duty. While I was trying to find Cardeur. In a word, Barone, I got clouted cold by someone I didn't see five minutes after you made that phone call to Miss Zaralis after leaving here yesterday. Don't tell me you didn't make that call?'

He smiled like I was a kid, and I had to really put the pressure on to hold my temper in place.

'I am afraid, *monsieur*, that I must tell you that I did not make any phone call to Zara,' he said. 'I did not call her until the early evening, and there was no answer.'

I looked at him hard to see if he was lying. He kept smiling politely right back at me, and somehow I felt that his statement had been on the up and up. I felt a little foolish because I'd sort of been half wondering if in some way that phone call could be linked up with my being clouted cold in a taxicab shortly after.

'Okay, forget it,' I said. And because I sure meant it, 'But I'd like to know just who *did* knock me for the blackout!'

Barone nodded as he gave me a very sympathetic smile.

'And we would like to know who killed Maurice,' he said. 'You have asked us, so now I ask you. Who do you think killed him, eh?'

I made like I was thinking that one over real seriously. Actually, I was debating whether or not to try and pull something out of a hat. I mean, tried and true methods are fine when they work. And so is the dogged kind of plugging away that Bierman goes in for mostly. But me, I like to pull things out of the air, and toss them into people's faces to see what happens. If anything.

'My hunch,' I told him, 'is somebody by the name of Herbert Varney.'

17

Well, I had pulled it out of the thin air and tossed it right into their faces. So I sat waiting for things to happen, and trying to catch their expressions all at the same time. I caught two of them, Barone's and Parkus'. Both blanks. I couldn't catch Goldilocks', though. She had buried her face in her hands and was weeping some more.

'Herbert Varney?' Barone said, pronouncing the name slowly to see how it felt coming off his tongue. 'Who is this Herbert Varney?'

'I don't know,' I said. 'Ever know anybody by that name? Say in France during the war?'

He looked at me sharply, his eyes all screwed up. Then he shook his head. 'No. No one by that name. But in the underground, one did not use his correct name. No. I did not know a Herbert Varney.'

I looked quickly at Parkus and hoisted an inquiring brow. He shook his head along with his grin.

'Not that I recall, Barnes,' he said. 'Nobody in my outfit by that name.'

'By the way, how long have you been out?' I asked.

'Not half enough,' he shot right back. 'Why?'

'Just interested,' I grunted. 'Got a job yet?'

His grin became fixed, and his eyes hardened a little. Then he gave with a short chuckle. 'Nope,' he said. 'I've got a piece of my pay in the bank. Plenty of time.'

'Don't blame you,' I said when I saw I was getting noplace. And then I looked at weeping Goldilocks. 'How about you, Gol . . . Miss Zaralis?' I caught myself in time. 'Do you, or did you, know anybody by that name?'

She lifted her head slowly and looked at me like a punch-drunk doll. 'No, the name I do not know,' she said. 'At least I do not think so. But my head! There is such an ache. You must pardon me . . . it has been so very much. I . . . '

She let the rest go. Rather, she finished

198

it with a little feeble movement of one hand. Henri Barone was on his feet in an instant.

'But of course, Zara!' he soothed her. 'You must rest. You must have sleep. It has been such a terrible blow. We will go at once. I will phone you later. Perhaps then you will be feeling a little better, eh?'

'Perhaps, Henri.' She smiled wanly and gave him her hand. 'But there is something. I still have you and Andy for my good friends. Do, Henri. Please call me later. Perhaps a quiet dinner some place? Just the three of us, eh?'

She went on talking, but I heard hardly any of it. I was too fascinated by the very smooth and easy performance that was being acted out right before my eyes. I mean, she had linked an arm with Barone, and one with Parkus, and was guiding them toward the apartment door. Yes sir! Right to the door and through it, just like I was some other guy in another state. Even when it came to me that Barone was going out the door owing me the other thousand for having found Cardeur dead or alive, the realization didn't seem important at all!

When she had closed the door on them, turned, and was starting back, I got set for the rushing and the gushing. The lady, however, crossed me up. She went by me and sat down on the divan. Her glass was empty, and so was mine, but she didn't seem to notice. Me, I can stand certain things just so long.

'What was the idea of that?' I demanded.

'Of that?' she echoed with a little quizzical smile.

I leaned forward, arms resting on my knees. 'The headache gag, and giving them the rush,' I said evenly. Then quickly, 'Did you, or did you not?'

She sat up straight, eyes wide. 'What?' she got out. Then with a frown, 'I am sorry, but I do not understand all kinds of the American talk.'

'If you're as crazy about Cardeur as Barone said, I should think you'd want to be alone,' I said. 'In other words, did you or did you not go for him that much?'

She thought that over, and then smiled broadly. 'My sweet Gerry, I think you try to break my heart, no?' she said.

'The idea hadn't occurred to me,' I grunted, and had the faint feeling that I was floundering. 'What do you mean?'

She didn't reply for a moment. First she lifted her two hands and gave each a little wave that took in the room; the whole apartment for that matter.

'All these nice things,' she said. 'Maurice could not give these to me. So you think Maurice is most jealous of René? He is so jealous that he decides he will kill René. So I find out that Maurice has killed René and that makes me very, very mad? I must punish Maurice because now René cannot pay for all these nice things? He is dead. So I punish Maurice, no? I kill him, too? It is the way you think, yes?'

I didn't give her an answer until I had mixed a drink for myself. And then I had to postpone it because she asked for one, too.

'Exactly the way I think, Goldilocks.' I grinned at her. 'But I don't think I'll call the cops yet. A couple of other things I want to find out first. One of them, the

Mr. X in this thing.'

'The Mr. X, Gerry?'

'Herbert Varney,' I said, and watched her.

She frowned, had some of her drink, and frowned some more. 'Who is this Herbert Varney?' she asked, still holding the frown, a perplexed one. 'Did René tell you about him when you talked at that so very awful party?'

I grinned, and couldn't stop it from working up into a chuckle. 'It seems there wasn't anybody at that brawl who didn't see DeFoe and me in a huddle! But, nope. DeFoe didn't mention that name.'

'Then who?' she asked petulantly. 'All this I cannot understand.'

'A little bird, but skip it,' I said. 'Tell me this — what did Gordon Parrish ever do to you?'

Bingo, and go collect the prize, Barnes! From sticky, sweet petulance to the flaming-eyed tigress in nothing flat. Damned if she didn't scare me . . . a little.

'Hold it!' I warned, and half lifted a hand. 'I was just interested why, that's all.'

She slowly put down her drink on the coffee table, folded her hands on her crossed knees, and looked at me out of eyes that didn't even see me.

'I will tell you,' she said, and there was no baby doll in *that* voice. 'I will tell you just one of many things, so that you will understand. It was in Paris. The second year of the war. Parrish was the . . . what you call, leader of our unit. He was in love with me, but I do not love him at all. He try so very hard, but always I refuse. I laugh at him. The others see me laugh. Parrish . . . he is a little like René. He cannot stand the laughter. So he try to have me fall into the hands of the Nazi Gestapo in Paris. Maurice finds out. It is Maurice who saves my life. He saves me from the Gestapo. I wish to kill Parrish when I find out. But it is impossible. Parrish is a swine, but he is also a . . . a . . . what you call, key man. It is to kill the Nazis that is the most important. So I do nothing. But Parrish? Perhaps one day I will kill him. I would so like to very much. You understand now, eh?'

Knowing what I did of Parrish, I

couldn't do anything else but nod. A little absently perhaps, because while she poured out her little tale, thoughts were coming and going in bunches inside my head.

'Just a pal,' I said. 'But he must have known about you and Cardeur, didn't he? And maybe you and René, too?'

'But yes,' she said simply. 'We were all of the underground. There were no secrets such as that.'

'Just one clubby family, eh?' I murmured. 'Then maybe you can tell me this. From here, it doesn't make sense. Seems to me, considering, that Parrish would have been tickled pink to have DeFoe and Cardeur go at each other's throats. Yet he helped me break it up. Why?'

I was a little surprised when I impulsively held my breath while I waited for her to come up with the answer. I did, though, and then let it out in a disappointed sigh.

'I do not know,' she said with a shake of her head. 'Perhaps he did not wish there to be fighting at the party.'

'Nuts! Look, Goldilocks!' I said,

tight-lipped. 'Maybe you folks in the underground think nothing at all about a couple of killings. Over here we look at it different. We don't like killings at all. Not even nice ones. Suppose you think hard and come up with what's behind it, eh?'

If it registered, it certainly didn't show in her face. 'Perhaps if you give me the explanation, Gerry?' she murmured.

As a starter for that, I held up my right hand with the thumb and second finger folded. 'DeFoe and Cardeur, both dead,' I said. 'They didn't kill each other. Somebody else did. Who? *I* have an idea. Why? *I* haven't that idea, yet. Over you? Maybe. What do you think?'

She started to speak, seemed to decide it not worth the effort, and let it go. She only shook her head in a dazed sort of way, and looked at me with her baby-blue eyes. I let mine harden some.

'It all could put you in a very tough spot, Goldilocks,' I said.

She blinked rapidly, and opened and closed her mouth a couple of times. 'Me?' she was able to get out. 'You mean . . . you think . . . the police . . . ?'

'Not the cops yet,' I interrupted. 'But me, maybe. How does this sound? Cardeur can't stand thinking about you and DeFoe anymore. He plays wire-man with DeFoe's neck. That leaves you. But he doesn't want to kill you. So that leaves the French way of beating up a lady. He comes here and tosses pepper in your eyes before you can see who it is. He scratches and kicks you some, and beats it. A sort of that's-for-nothing-now-look-out idea. Later *he* comes up dead. What would *you* think, Goldilocks?'

The baby-doll stare wasn't anywhere to be seen. My cockeyed reasoning had planted fear; planted it deep. Her face paled, and she licked her lips several times. She started to put out a hand toward me, then pulled it back.

'But I would never kill Maurice!' she said in a frenzied voice. 'Never! He . . . But you are a fool! A fool, do you not see?'

'Why am I a fool?' I asked.

'Because it is so impossible!' she cried. 'Lieutenant Bierman will tell you. I am so frightened that he gets the lady in the next apartment to stay with me the rest of the night. She is willing, and I am glad for her to stay. Do you not see? I am here in *this* apartment all the night. I . . . I am very disappointed. I think perhaps you will go away. No! I do not think that I like you at all, now!'

I shrugged, sighed, and stood up. I went over and patted her shoulder. She didn't lift her head.

'Okay, I'm sorry, Goldilocks,' I said. 'After all, it was just a thought. Heels like me get lots of thoughts. You'd be surprised at the kinds. Sorry about Cardeur, too. Now you go get that rest. Some night I'll buy you a dinner, and try to get you to forgive. Bye, baby.'

I didn't wait to see if my few words had softened her any. I had come in strictly on business, and I went out the same way. But when I was down on the sidewalk and debating my next move, a question suddenly occurred to me. I mean, just *why* had she given Barone and Parkus the rush, and kept me there? It certainly hadn't been for the reason *you'd* be inclined to think, that was a cinch!

18

My sidewalk debate ended in a compromise. I took a cab and went to the office. If I was lucky, there might be something there connected with the couple of phone calls I'd made to Washington, D.C. At that point in the jigsaw puzzle, I needed a break. A great big break. Either one of them, or both of them, could give me that break. At least I thought they could. And so I had all of my fingers mentally crossed when I unlocked my office door and pushed it open.

The first thing I saw was the yellow Western Union envelope on the floor at my feet. It had been slipped through the mail slot in the door. I picked it up quickly and saw at once that it was dated Washington, D.C. I kicked the door shut with my heel and hurried over to my desk and sat down. This was it, at long last ... I hoped, and prayed. For a brief moment, I just stared at the sealed flap;

then I worked a fingertip under one corner and ripped it along. I pulled out the wire, and saw that it was from one of the lads I'd phoned. I read the wire, swore out loud, and read it again. It said:

BEFORE ASKING PAULA, WHAT WOULD YOU DO FIRST? LUCK!

TED

That was exactly what the wire said, and after reading it six more times I was still spinning out of control. I stared at it, glared at it, and swore at it, but that didn't help any. The single ribbon of typed words stuck to the sheet just mocked my every thought and mood. I knew that it wasn't any gag. And then I wasn't so sure. I swore some more, and grabbed for the phone to call Washington. But something seemed to make me drop my hand and leave the phone where it was. Maybe because I was certain my friend, Ted, didn't go in for gags of that type. He was top-drawer in the FBI. Strictly not the fooling type.

And so I stared at the wire some more.

I tried to figure out if it was in some sort of code. But after ten minutes of getting nowhere, I gave that up. Yet something had to be there, if I could only make sense out of it. After some calm and careful thinking, I realized that because of his position, Ted couldn't come right out with details. The best he could do was give me a hint. It was up to me to figure it out. Ten to one he'd probably hang right up if I called him.

I don't know why, but I looked at my desk clock. The hands said twenty-eight minutes after two. I vaguely realized that I could do with some lunch. I didn't do anything about it, though. That screwy telegram from Washington, D.C. held me pinned to my chair. I stared at it some more, and slowly little by little I went stark-raving nuts.

And then, suddenly, when the last thread of the Barnes' sanity was about to snap, the tiny light came on way in back of my brain. It grew and grew like the headlight of an onrushing locomotive, and then blew up silently as I let out a happy yell and smacked a hand palm first on the desk.

'Eureka!' was what came out of my mouth. 'Got it, so help me. You're a louse, Ted, to make me sweat, but I love you!'

After those few words, I calmed down and did some more thinking. A great big hunk of the jigsaw puzzle was in place to stay. But there was another big piece that should fit right alongside of it. I mean, the piece in the form of that sheet of paper covered with Herbert Varney signatures I'd found in Cardeur's waste-paper basket. To help along my thinking, I unlocked the center desk drawer and took out the sheet. And that chain ring of keys, too. As a thought came to me, I studied the keys one by one. When I was through, I hadn't found what I'd hoped to; but frankly, hadn't expected to.

I pushed the keys to one side and studied the paper filled with the same signature. More than ever, I was positive that it was the results of efforts to improve a signature until the forgery and the original would match. Sure, I figured that out, but it didn't tell me anything. If only I'd found attempts to practice René DeFoe's signature, then maybe . . .

A sudden blinding thought crowded out all the others. I sat there stunned for a moment, and then I felt very foolish for not having come up with that thought hours before. A look at my desk clock told me I had just eight minutes before the bank where René DeFoe had opened his fifty-thousand-dollar account would close for the day. I used up two of those eight minutes getting out of the office and taking the elevator down. Luck was with me, because somebody was just paying off a cab as I dashed out onto the sidewalk. I grabbed it, and waved a five-dollar bill in front of the driver's face. He earned the five with a couple of minutes to spare.

As luck would have it, I had once years ago had an account with that bank, so I knew my way around. The safety deposit vaults were below ground. I hurried down the stairs and over to the grill-doors. No one was ahead of me, so that was a help, too. The guard looked at me and smiled politely. I hesitated just long enough to breathe a quick, fervent prayer. Then I smiled politely at the guard and made as though to take a keyring from my pocket.

'Herbert Varney,' I told him.

He nodded, repeated the name, and shoved a signature card under the grill-shelf for me to sign. Then he pulled open the file card cabinet drawer and started thumbing through it. I made as though to pick up the pen. I did it very slowly. And just as slowly I dipped it in the inkwell. By then, the guard had stopped thumbing through the cards. He had one card half pulled out. He looked at it, and then at me. The smile slowly left his face, and his features began to harden. I put down the pen, snapped my fingers, and started fishing through my pockets.

'Something wrong, mister?' The guard's voice was like ice cubes dropping on more ice cubes. And his eyes on me were twice as cold.

'Damn it to hell, yes!' I said in savage exasperation. 'Varney forgot to give me that letter of identification. Now I've got to go back and . . . '

I mumbled it to a full stop as I turned and hurried back up the stairs, with the guard's iced-oyster eyes following me every step I went up. When I was at the top and out of his sight, I slowed down and gave the Barnes several unseen pats on the back. My think-box was certainly paying off today in big chunks. Then a hand was on my arm, and a cordial voice in my ear.

'Why, hello, Mr. Barnes! Haven't seen you in here in years. Anything I can do for you?'

I turned my head to look at a pleasant enough smiling face that didn't mean anything to me for a moment. And then it did. Out of the dim, dim past came the memory that he was Jones, or Smith, or maybe Kelley. Anyway, at that time he had been a third assistant vice president, or something. Probably now he owned the joint. I shook his hand, and I also shook my head.

'Why, no, thank you,' I said. 'I was to meet a friend here, but . . . '

There I stopped because the think-box was really giving out with it.

'Yes there is, too.' I smiled at him. 'I wonder if you could tell me something?'

'I'd be only too glad to, Mr. Barnes,' he bubbled. Then quickly, 'If I know, of course. What is it?'

'Could a man, or woman, produce one identity and take out a checking account,' I said, 'and then, say a day or two later, go downstairs and rent a savings deposit box under another name? Could that be done?'

He didn't answer directly. First he had to squint up his eyes, purse his lips, and gravely stroke his undershot chin with his right forefinger.

'Not in *this* bank, Mr. Barnes,' he finally told me. 'But no doubt it could be done in some banks where they are . . . er . . . far less careful. Why do you ask?'

'Oh, just to settle a little bet.' I grinned, and pumped his hand. 'Thanks. Thanks a lot.'

I left him there squinting up his eyes again, and going after his undershot chin some more. The main-door guard had to open up to let me out. I went out into the sunshine. And it struck me as being the nicest sunshine I had ever seen. Yes sir! Unless I was completely off the beam, which of course could be, Mr. Jones, or Smith, or Kelley, or whatever his name was, had certainly overestimated his bank!

And then without warning, the beautiful sunlight snuffed out. Figuratively speaking, of course. What actually happened was that a taxi drifted slowly by, and seated in back, where he thought I couldn't see him, was 'Sore-Jaw' Franz Eurlich! One look at him and I did a fatheaded thing. I shifted into high from a standing start and raced out toward the cab. A couple of cars missed me by inches, and I missed my target by a couple of feet. Two feet more and I would have yanked open that cab door and leaped inside. But Eurlich had barked at the cab driver, and the sudden burst of speed left me in the middle of the street looking like I was shaking hands with thin air. Horns blared in my ears, and then a big traffic cop was towering over me.

'You crazy, or just drunk, mister?' he bulled out. 'Didn'tcha see he had a passenger?'

'Yeah,' I grunted. 'That was why I tried to make it.'

'Huh?'

I didn't say any more. I walked away

from that cop leaving him growling words which, no doubt, he had already growled at a dozen other jay-dopes since coming on duty. When I reached the sidewalk, I also reached the decision that, murder or not, I had to eat. So I went up a couple of blocks, one over eastward, and found a little place where the food was good, and the customers the strong silent type.

When I came out, it was something after four o'clock. The inner Barnes was quite content. And, as a matter of fact, the mental Barnes was feeling pretty good too, thank you. I had done me an awful lot of serious thinking, and some guessing. And the result was that I felt sure that not many more pieces were needed to be fitted into place to give me the whole picture. Anyway, it seemed that way to me as I popped into a cigar store and called Paula's apartment.

No answer for the third time. I looked at my watch. Four-thirty. No use, now, calling the couple of places where I might have found her earlier. My best bet was the Biltmore Cocktail Lounge. Dropping in there around five was a daily custom of ours, whether together or alone. That is, unless something else had popped up. Well, nothing had popped up for me, so I took a cab cross-town to have an early one, or two, and wait to see if something had popped up for Paula. Or seemingly had, I mean. After what Bierman had told me, maybe she'd stay away on purpose today. Especially after my not going through with the usual routine yesterday. Which I was unable to, being very, very unconscious at the time!

I had no sooner walked under the clock than I saw her. Sitting right at our usual table, and with . . . guess who? None other than Gordon Parrish! I was so flattened that Nick, gliding to my side, had to speak three times and then touch my arm. I looked down at him for an instant, not seeing him. Then I did.

'Hi, Nick,' I said, with not too much life in it. 'They been here long?'

With Nick, I didn't have to point or even nod the direction. He knew.

'About half an hour, Mr. Barnes,' he said. Then quietly, 'The usual?'

'The usual, but a double,' I said, and

started threading through the tables toward them. Paula saw me first, and smiled brightly. Relief, or spite, I didn't know.

'Hello, darling!' she said. 'You're early, too. Did you have a nice trip?'

I didn't even look at Parrish. Not yet. I grinned, bent over and kissed Paula.

'A lovely trip, lovely,' I said. 'You should have been along. Hello, Parrish. Eurlich all right now?'

I was looking at him then. His ugly mug went very red, and then worked itself into a smile. 'Yes, quite all right, Mr. Barnes,' he said, and hitched over a little to make more room for me. 'And I would like to say that he got what he deserved. I apologize again.'

'What's this?' Paula broke in. 'Somebody apologizing to you, Gerry? Seems to me it's often the other way round.'

That was the tip-off. Paula was on that high horse of hers still, and riding it hell for leather. I didn't even look at her. I still looked at Parrish.

'Forget it,' I said, and tried to make it good-natured. 'He's just the impulsive type, I guess. Besides, who am I to blame you for having me shadowed? Certainly not. You'd paid out money, and were entitled to protect your investment in whatever way you thought best. Right?'

He knew that I was actually spitting in his eye, but he couldn't do a single thing about it other than to keep smiling and take it.

'Well, that's a very nice way of putting it, sir,' he said. Then, with a glance Paula's way, he said, 'As a matter of fact, Mr. Barnes, that's the reason you find me in such charming company. I mean, I've been trying to find you ever since you left in order to explain more fully about Franz's shock at the news, so that you wouldn't continue to be offended by so disgraceful an episode.'

I certainly felt like telling the lying cluck that *last night's* episode had offended me a hell of a sight more. But I let it ride. I didn't think it time yet to bring up things like that. However, I didn't let him off with just another smile.

'I'm never in here until this time any afternoon,' I said. 'I'm usually at my office or my apartment.'

'But Mr. Barnes,' he got out as his face became the color of an underdone steak; one that had been run over by a tank, 'I phoned both your office, and then your apartment, and . . . '

Paula's heel dug into my shin as she spoke. 'And then he called me, Gerry,' she said. 'Lord knows *I* didn't know where you were. It's been a long time since you left to make a *visit* yesterday noon, you know! So I told Mr. Parrish you usually dropped in here around five. And he was nice enough to invite me to join him and wait.'

At that moment, Nick came with my drink. I looked at Paula's half empty, and Parrish's all the way empty, and nodded at Nick. He went away. I took a deliberately long pull at mine, and set it on the little table with a sigh. A contented one.

'Well, all's well with the world,' I said in my brightest voice. 'Very much all well, for me.'

Parrish almost slid off his chair, he leaned forward so quickly. 'You mean, Mr. Barnes . . . ? You mean you've found the murderer?'

I looked at him blank-faced. 'Which murder?' I said.

And he looked at me like a hooked fish trying to get air. 'I beg your pardon?' he gulped.

'I said which murder?' I repeated.

'Why . . . why, both!' he managed. 'You know who killed René DeFoe, and also Maurice Cardeur?'

I continued to give him the blank face. Then I shook my head slowly. 'No, I don't,' I said. And with a to-hell-with-that shrug, I added, 'That's for the police. Right now I'm quite content to know *why*. The motive, to be technical.'

19

If my remark startled Parrish any, he was clever enough to cover it up so I couldn't tell. As a matter of fact, though, I could only watch him for a couple of split seconds. Paula shot out a hand, gripped mine, and I was forced to give her my attention. Her eyes were big and wide.

'You know why René DeFoe, and this Maurice Cardeur, were murdered, Gerry?' she exclaimed. 'Tell me.'

I frowned and shook my head. 'The things you ask in public,' I countered. Then with a gesture, I asked, 'What do you think I've been doing in the last thirty hours or so?'

That was a mistake, and I knew it the instant it was off my tongue. Paula stiffened, and her eyes became very dangerous.

'*That* is what I'd like to know most of all,' she snapped. 'I'll bet it wasn't *all* work and no play!'

That would get us nowhere, except in each other's hair, so I simply looked hurt and turned to Parrish. 'Incidentally, I'm glad you did find me,' I said. 'Truth of the matter is I called your place a couple of times, but there was no answer. There's a couple of things I want to ask you.'

He twisted his ugly face into a smile, but his eyes were as sharp as a pistol shot. 'I only hope I can answer them, Mr. Barnes,' he said.

I held off while Nick set down their refills.

'Counting out DeFoe,' I finally said, 'who would you say was mad enough at Cardeur to want to kill him?'

The first part of his answer was a dry chuckle, and a little helpless shake of his head.

'I told you before, in this very place,' he said with a wave at the lounge, 'that we of the underground had hundreds of enemies. And many of them are still our enemies today. We . . . '

'Yes, I remember,' I cut in, and watched him closely. 'But I understand you had very few secrets from each other. Maybe you can narrow down the field to two or three, eh?'

He looked at me a long time, and I did not like the way he looked at me.

'If DeFoe were alive and Maurice dead, the answer to that would be simple,' he said slowly. 'But they are both dead, so it is very confusing.'

'To put it mildly,' I couldn't help murmuring. Then straight from the shoulder I asked, 'What about that lad by the name of Herbert Varney? Think he hated Cardeur that much?'

My fishing trip was a flop. At least as far as the expression on his face, and in his eyes, was concerned. He simply looked at me, and then slowly knitted his brows and wrinkled up his forehead.

'I am afraid I cannot answer that,' he said, 'because I do not know of anyone by that name. You have met him?'

'I think DeFoe knew him well,' I said. 'At least, the digging around I've done causes me to come up with that belief. Sure you don't know him?'

'Very sure, Mr. Barnes. I am very sure that I have never heard that name in my whole life.'

I sighed, grinned, shrugged, and toyed

with my drink a couple of moments. Although he didn't know it, Parrish had admitted something I suspected but wanted confirmed.

'What were the reasons?' he suddenly cut into my thoughts. 'The reasons René and Maurice were killed.'

'Reason, not reasons,' I corrected.

And then for a second or two I hesitated. Should I let him know for sure I wasn't just casting blindly hither and yon? Or should I make it look like I was? I decided in favor of the former. I decided it might be a good idea to give Gordon Parrish something to think about.

'A very high-priced reason, too,' I said, looking at him. 'I don't know the exact figure. Maybe a million dollars, or maybe five million. However, I'll find out exactly in due time.'

I'd scored! He tried to look all confused, but he was just as quick to hide his face in his drink. During the moment of silence Paula came into the conversation again.

'Can't I play, too?' she said sweetly, bittersweetly. 'Or is this for men only?'

'Certainly not.' I grinned at her. 'Who do you think killed DeFoe and Cardeur?'

'That's easy, if they were friends of your precious little painted doll!' she came right back at me.

'You mean Zara?' I murmured, grinning more.

I loved all the little storm warnings that unfurled in her eyes.

'Oh? So *now* it's Zara!'

'Her first name, believe it or not,' I said. 'And, yes, they were friends of Zara's. So?'

You could have picked up her icy words off the floor one by one.

'So they killed each other. She's the type to drive men to that. Even *supposedly* grown-up men!'

I felt that I had won the round, so I dropped it. Parrish had taken his ugly map out of his drink and was watching us with what looked like confused anger.

'You know Miss Zaralis, don't you?' I asked him.

'Why yes, yes, of course,' he got out after a moment. 'She was with us in the underground, as you probably know.'

'All about it,' I said, and watched him squirm . . . only he didn't. 'What do you think of her?'

'Think of her?' He seemed to be stalling. 'What do you mean, Mr. Barnes?'

I made a little gesture to indicate I really wasn't quite sure just what I meant. 'Her work in the underground,' I said. 'Was she good? You know — capable, brave, and all that sort of thing? And, incidentally, did she work with Cardeur much?'

He had the answer all ready for me. 'She did much for the success of the movement,' he said. 'I mean, so I have been told. I barely knew her over there. Some of us, you know, were simply numbers to each other.'

'Parrish, I think very much that you are a cockeyed liar!'

No, I did not say that out loud, but I certainly thought it as I stared at him. And I wouldn't be at all surprised but that he deduced exactly what I was thinking. I decided it might be a good idea to stir the boiling pot a little.

'Do you know who she thinks killed

Cardeur?' I asked.

He looked at me blankly for an instant. 'You have asked her?' he wanted to know.

'Sure,' I said pleasantly. 'How am I going to find out things if I don't ask questions? Believe it or not, Zara thinks *you* killed Cardeur.'

A swift punch to his lumpy potato-shaped nose would have produced an identical effect. His head went back, and he blinked. He started to go overboard with seething rage but caught himself in time. Those people in the underground were certainly good actors. But I guess they had to be, when you come to think of it.

'*Me?*' he finally panted out. 'She . . . Zara told you I killed *Maurice?*'

I kept shooting at him. 'You know Henri Barone, don't you?'

'Yes, but . . . ?'

I wouldn't let him finish. 'I think he thinks you killed DeFoe, too.'

His mouth worked, but he couldn't say anything. He could only look at me, at Paula, and at the lounge floor for maybe a great big hole.

'I found out something,' I said, then changed it. 'I mean, the police found out something. Both garroting wires used come off the same spool. Or maybe it was a coil. A real good search of this place and that place might turn up the rest of it. What do you think?'

He looked at me, and he could have yelled out loud what he was thinking. Which, of course, he didn't. But I knew damn well my guess was right. Gordon Parrish was thinking of a certain room where I had been 'entertained' last night, and wishing like hell that his boys hadn't been so slipshod about things.

'I think you are mad, completely mad, Mr. Barnes!' was what he actually did say. 'It is unthinkable that I would do that to either René or Maurice! If people would tell the truth, they would tell you that I loved them both, as brothers. *Mademoiselle* Grant, I am very sorry. I have an appointment. You will pardon me for leaving, yes?'

He was on his feet, and bowing all over the place, as he spoke the last. I wanted to laugh, and when I glanced at Paula I thought I saw more than just a twinkle in her eyes.

'Of course, Mr. Parrish,' she assured him. 'It's been very interesting meeting you.'

He bowed again, and ignored Nick standing by with the check for the drinks before I arrived. I gave Nick the wink, and he wandered away. Parrish stepped by me without so much as a look. I let him go a few steps, and then stopped him.

'Oh, just a minute, Parrish.'

He turned and tried to coat me with ice all over. 'Yes?' Very, very flat-voiced.

I took the few steps toward him. 'I'd like you to take a message to Eurlich, if you will?' I said.

He stiffened a little, and his face tightened a little, too. 'A message?' he echoed.

'That's right,' I said. 'Tell Eurlich to please keep his taxicab off whatever street I happen to be on. Thanks, and bye, Parrish.'

I turned and went back to Paula. By the time I was seated, Gordon Parrish was under the lounge clock on his way out! And thinking, no doubt, lots of dandy things.

20

'And that, I think, is that,' I murmured, and picked up my drink.

Paula took her lovely eyes off the retreating figure of Parrish and turned them on me. 'As your prospective wife, darling,' she said, 'I suppose I shouldn't butt in on your business affairs. But might I ask if there goes your killer?'

'You might,' I said to her, 'but I'd rather take up this prospective wife thing. Says who?'

She gave me a little smile, and in that moment I wished more than anything that I could really convince myself we wouldn't be throwing dishes and carving knives after the first six months, or a year at the most.

'You say the nicest things to make a gal happy, darling,' she said.

I shook my head. We'd been all over that a hundred million times. 'Your drink's getting cold,' I said. 'What did

Parrish have to say before I turned up?'

She ignored her drink and my question.

'Ever since you took up this crazy business you have no business in, you've made me a very lonely something,' she said. 'Did you know that?'

'Let's not, precious,' I said quietly. 'Wanting to try it has been in my blood ever since diaper days. I'm getting my chance at last. I . . . Dammit, Paula, murder and marriage just don't mix. You'd stay up nights waiting, and worrying yourself sick!'

'As if I don't know!' she said scornfully. And then with one of the patent-applied-for Paula Grant quick changes, she said with a sigh, 'Okay, okay. Let's talk about you, then. What does the other guy look like?'

'Huh?' I echoed, not thinking.

'Your face and head, darling. The lumps. Did you forget to lead with your fists again?'

'I couldn't; they were tied!' I blurted out.

That was a bad slip. She would now fire questions a dozen in a bunch, and I had other things on my mind. But I couldn't begin speaking fast enough to stop her first one. First bunch, I mean.

'Why were your hands tied? Who tied them? When did this happen? And what did you do about it?'

'Hold it, hold it!' I tried to stop her with raised hands. 'I don't know. For sure, anyway. Look, you want to help me with this thing?'

'Help you with what thing? Parrish is your killer, isn't he? Why don't you have him arrested? *Well, why don't you?*'

The last was because I was hurriedly seeking refuge in my drink. 'If you'll only shut that beautiful mouth a moment!' I pleaded. 'Now, what did you and Parrish have to say to each other?'

'None of your damned business! And I think he's rather fascinating, even if he isn't good-looking.'

'So you won't help?' I said wearily.

'Why should I?' she demanded, and tossed her flaming sunset-crowned head. 'You're the one who's playing at being detective. And from those lumps, I'd say the others play just a little too hard for you.'

'They promised not to anymore,' I

snapped. 'Look, Paula, maybe you can and maybe you can't help me. I don't know yet. Fact is, there's a whole lot of things I don't know yet. Well?'

'Maybe I could help if you'd tell me all about it,' she said. 'Whatever it's all about.'

I shook my head. 'It'd take too long,' I parried. 'But when it's all cleaned up, sure.'

'Thanks,' she bit off. 'Like the *last* time, eh? Just the big silent clam until your horse is home. You can go fry something, Mr. Barnes!'

'*I* won't!' I snapped back at her. 'But I think the state *will*, and in the not too distant future, either.'

'Once over lightly, please?' she said with a frown. 'The state?'

'The state,' I said soberly. 'Cops, and fellows like me, just do the groundwork, and tuck in all the loose ends. It's the state that sits the people in the electric chair.'

Paula stared at me a moment, and then shivered. Some of the peach bloom left her cheeks, and fear crowded into her eyes. I hoped it was fear for my welfare. It was.

'Don't talk like that, darling, please!' she said with a little catch in her voice. 'It gives me pictures of what might happen before the state had a chance to do that to somebody. Parrish, for instance. That face. Ugh!'

'You said it was fascinating,' I told her.

'No.' She shook her head. 'His manner, and speech. Never his face. Nick almost fainted. I'm sure I don't know what he must think.'

'Nick is used to people who go slumming in the zoo,' I said gravely. 'But we're off the track. Will you, or won't you, answer my question?'

'Marry you, Gerry?' She glowed. 'Why, darling, this is so . . . ' She cut off the rest short, reached out quickly, and covered my hand with hers. 'Sorry, pal, I'm really such a so-and-so,' she said softly. 'You'll have to give me more time, that's all. To get used to the new you. Now, what do you want to know?'

I didn't tell her at once. I covered her hand with my other one and pressed hard. And I thought that maybe when I cracked this case, and made it two straight, with a batting percentage of a thousand, I'd . . . But I didn't finish the thought.

'Only what you and Parrish talked about,' I said. 'If anything.'

'Well, it was mostly this and that,' she said. 'He was busting a gut to be polite, but I could tell he had a lot on his mind.'

'He's got more than that now, I think,' I murmured. 'Did he tell you about Cardeur?'

'Yes,' she replied with a little shiver. 'My God, how horrible. Gerry, who . . . ? Sorry; you're not talking, are you? Well, he talked about it, and about DeFoe, too, as though he half hoped that I'd break in with an item here and there. Naturally, I didn't know any items, but I think he thought I did. I wouldn't like to meet Mr. Parrish on a dark street late at night.'

'Tried to pump you about me, huh?' I murmured.

'Yes.' Paula nodded. 'Very anxious to know what progress you'd made. Just as though you'd told me. But he certainly had his nerve thinking. I mean, even if you had.'

I grinned, and pressed her hand some more. 'Wish I did have time to give it all to you, beautiful,' I said. 'But it's still slightly cockeyed to me.'

'Ah!' Paula let out, but all wrapped up in a sad note. 'So I dine alone again, eh? And I go to the movies alone, too? Why do heels have to be such perfect people underneath?'

'Tomorrow night, I buy you the town,' I said. 'I hope. But I have too much homework tonight.'

'Short washed-out blonde, and dumpy in the wrong places?' she sneered at me.

'You don't know how nicely green eyes go with your hair.' I grinned at her. 'But no, Zara has cast me out forever. I don't think the lady likes me anymore.'

'Nuts!' Paula snorted. 'There isn't enough room in that empty head of hers to hold that much sense!'

I grinned, and then tried to bite down on my tongue to stop the words coming off. I knew I was a fool to ask, but I had to just the same.

'Speaking of nothing at all,' I put it casually, 'where were you last night around eleven thirty?'

There, it was out, and I certainly felt an awful cheap fool for having asked it. But I guess Paula thought I wanted to know because maybe I had phoned her at that time. Anyway, she didn't bristle, or jump at, any second meanings.

'At the movies with Beth Price,' she said. 'Call her and check, if you like. Where were *you*?'

I *would* throw boomerangs! 'In a room,' I grunted.

'Interesting! What room? And where?'

It was no use trying the quick switch to another topic. It just wouldn't work. 'I don't know,' I told her honestly. 'I was out. Unconscious, I mean.'

'Oh, is there a difference?' She shot it at me tight-lipped. 'You louse, Gerry Barnes! While I was worrying myself sick, you were drinking the spots dry with that — '

'The hell I was!' I cut her off. 'I was out because the human head can stand just so much of being belted from east to west, and west to east. If it'll make you feel any better, I left Zara's apartment at two o'clock in the afternoon, and I didn't see her again yesterday.'

'What about today, up until four thirty?' Paula demanded. 'Of course you didn't see her again today! Not much you didn't! And me . . . '

'Stop it!' I came close to shouting. 'I've worn this finger down to the first knuckle dialing your number, but you weren't in. Listen, if you think . . . Oh, skip it!'

I was tired, and my head ached, and I had too many things to do besides battle with Paula. Which would actually have been fun at any other time. And so I didn't voice any protest when she gathered up her things and pushed back her chair.

'Yes, let's both skip it,' she said. 'You need to be alone. Do call me when the balloon goes up. I love to throw rocks. Bye, Gerry.'

'Bye, darling,' I mumbled, and stared moodily at my half-finished drink.

For a few minutes after Paula had gone, I sat there feeling very sorry for Gerry Barnes. It just seemed that nobody could understand the things he was going through. The way he was working so hard. Putting pleasures behind him and giving all of himself to his task. And by then, I got around to realizing that I'd better give a little more if I wanted my team to win. I finished my drink, put a bill on the table, and walked toward the lobby. Nick watched me go like he was going to burst out in tears. He, of course, had seen Paula take off nose high, and was worried. His face brightened up like a Christmas tree, though, when I winked at him and flashed the think-nothing-of-it-pal sign.

In the lobby I went to the phone booths, got me a Manhattan directory, and took it into one of the booths with me. I sat down on the little stool and took out a slip of paper on which I had copied down from memory six of some ten addresses I had seen in the departed DeFoe's little black book. Then I went to work.

In the next half hour I had made six calls, and been connected on each one. To each person who took my call I asked the same question. I got five answers in a row that didn't help me at all. On the sixth and last call I got the answer I wanted. I thanked the person at the other end of the wire, hung up, and surrendered my booth to an impatient fat woman who tried to reduce me to a grease spot on the floor with a single look. But I felt so good I grinned at her, and tipped my hat.

'Madam,' I said, 'why are people born liars?'

'Young man, you're drunk!' she snapped, and almost caught four of my fingertips as she slammed the two-part door shut.

I thought it might help to make her statement correct. And then I told myself that it wouldn't help anything. That decided, I walked slowly down the long flight toward the Forty-Third Street entrance. The balloon could go up any time now, as far as I was concerned.

21

My friends still wouldn't believe me, even if I put both hands on a Bible, but it so happens that by nine thirty that night I was in my apartment, in my pajamas, and settled comfortably in my favorite chair. On the end table to my left were the evening papers, a couple of magazines, and a book I'd promised Paula I'd read. And on the end table to my right were a nice cold bottle of beer, a plate of crackers, and a slab of tangy cheese. To coin a phrase, I was going to spend a quiet evening at home.

The jigsaw puzzle was now all complete. That is, as far as my interest in it was concerned. All that remained was to make sure that the pieces remained stuck together, and justice prevailed. That would not be determined until tomorrow at the earliest. And so the thing for me to do was rest my weary brains and battered head, and be in a fit condition to pitch the last of the ninth, so to speak.

No, I wasn't exactly brimming over with quiet confidence. There were a couple of little things that gave me uneasy thoughts as I leaned back and gazed pensively at my living room ceiling. However, they were minor things, and when I checked over everything I did know, and would bet my last dime on, I didn't feel too bad. Anyway, there wasn't a thing I could do about anything until the morrow. And so, brushing it all to one side, I drank deep of my cold beer and reached for one of the papers.

And at that moment, my telephone on the table in the corner chose to ring. I stared at it coldly and shook my head.

'No, Paula, my love,' I murmured out loud. 'Some other night I'd love to very much. But tonight, no. The Barnes must get his rest.'

And the telephone rang again. I half rose from my chair, but sat right back again. It rang the third time, and I got up and walked over to it. At least I owed her the courtesy of answering it, so she'd know I was all right. So I picked up the phone and said: 'Hello, darling!'

And a split second later I felt very foolish, because a man's voice said: 'Who is this?'

And a half a split second after that I was all attention, because I had recognized Henri Barone's voice!

'This is Barnes,' I said. Then, with an apologetic laugh, 'I thought you were someone else, Barone. I . . . I'm expecting a call.'

'Oh,' he said, and a little disappointed it sounded. 'One of great importance, *monsieur?*'

'Well, not too important, I guess,' I told him. 'Why? What do you want?'

'I would like to see you, *Monsieur* Barnes,' he said. 'I would like to see you very much.'

I frowned, and looked over at my chair, and my beer, and my cheese and crackers. Definitely I did not want to share them with anybody. 'What about?' I asked. 'And, can't it keep until morning?'

'No, I am afraid no,' he said. 'Could you not come up here, *monsieur?* It is not so far.'

'Where's here?' I asked quickly.

He gave me an address in the One Hundred and Twenties, and way over west by the Hudson River. I got a little sore.

'Are you kidding?' I snapped. 'It so happens I'm ready for bed. Why should I chase way the hell up there? If it simply can't keep until morning, you come down here. I'll wait up thirty minutes for you.'

'One moment, I beg of you, *monsieur!*' he almost cried down the telephone wire. 'Do not be offended, but it is impossible for me to come down there. I have been hurt, *Monsieur* Barnes. My leg. But I must speak to you about . . . about Zara. You will come here, yes?'

I didn't say anything. Instead I did a lot of fast and furious thinking. So Henri Barone wanted to see me about Goldilocks? Did the guy think I was a dope? Did he think that the Barnes was a deaf, dumb, and blind dope? It would appear so.

'You are there, *monsieur?*' his anxious voice came into my ear.

'Yes, I'm here,' I told him. 'What about Zara?'

'I am sorry,' he said. 'It is impossible to

tell you over this telephone. But you will come, yes?'

I let him wait some more while I carefully weighed a thing or two. Maybe he was on the up and up. And maybe, too, he wanted to play spider to the Barnes fly. But then again, maybe . . .

'All right, Barone,' I said. 'I guess I can come, if you insist. What's . . . ?'

'I insist, and I also beg of you, *monsieur!*' he broke in on me.

'Okay, okay,' I stopped him. 'What's your apartment number, and floor?'

'It is the basement rear, *Monsieur* Barnes,' he said. 'You go down the passageway at the side of the building. It is just around at the back. There is a little light over the door. You will see. Do not bother to ring. Come right in, *monsieur*. I will be here waiting for you.'

'Okay,' I said again, and glanced at my desk clock. It said twenty of ten. 'I've got to dress, but I'll be there about ten thirty. Bye, now.'

I hung up while he was expressing his delight and his thanks. I stood with my hand still resting on the phone for a minute or so. To put it mildly, I was worried and perplexed. Barone's phone call had seemingly messed up the parade. It was completely out of line with the way I had carefully and skillfully, I thought, fitted all the jigsaw puzzle pieces together. Yes, I was either a complete dope, or else Henri Barone was the complete dope. But still and all . . .

'Nuts!' I said, and shook my head to break up the crazy merry-go-round of thoughts. 'There's a very good way to find out, Barnes!'

And with that, I went into the bedroom and got into some clothes. And the last thing I did before putting on my hat was to take my gun from its shoulder holster and slide the safety off. If perchance I was going to be needing it, I wanted it ready for instant use.

Riding uptown in the cab, I tried hard to figure out a reason, if any, why Barone should want to see me about Goldilocks. And I did a lot of thinking, too, about his injured leg. Had it been an accident, how bad, and that kind of thing. Barone was no little guy, and if he'd been in the underground he certainly would know how to take care of himself. However, big and little guys were all the same to a passing truck or a cowboy taxicab driver. They . . . I shook my head to clear it out. My rambling thoughts were dizzy, and were fast making me the same way.

A couple of blocks this side of my intended destination I paid off the cabby, and paused on the sidewalk to look around. The view across the Hudson to the Jersey side was very pretty. The lights on the boats riding at anchor seemed to wink at me, and Palisades Park was throwing a multi-tinted glow high up and outward in all directions.

On my side of the river, though, it wasn't so bright and cheerful. Very few lights at all. The folks in that section either went to bed early, or went out every night. True, there were a couple of lights here and there, but all in all it held very much of a gloomy note. Even the glow of the headlights tossed up from the cars passing to and fro on the West Side Express Highway didn't seem to break up the gloom any.

From force of habit, I stuck my hand under my jacket front and made sure my gun was resting loose and free in the holster. And then I started walking up the street. Barone's building wasn't much to look at. In fact, nothing at all compared with the twenty- or twenty-five-story buildings that flanked it on either side. It only pushed its way up some seven floors, and there it stopped. It looked almost as though the building contractor had suddenly run out of materials and said the hell with it.

The south side of the building was fitted snug to the wall of the next, but there was a small passageway to the rear on the other side just as Barone had said. It was an alley, and nothing more. A night-darkened, gloomy alley, but at least I could see that there were no potential murderers, or what have you, lurking in it. The glow from the light that was over Barone's door shed enough glow across the end to silhouette anything, or anyone, who might be in the alley.

I grinned a little sheepishly at the thoughts I had been thinking. After all, Barone would be just plain nuts to think he could lure me into some pitch-dark alley. Anyway, nothing was going to happen in that alley, that was a cinch.

And right there, the gods on high who like to watch dumb clucks stumble their way through life screamed out in high glee, and probably rolled over hugging themselves. I mean, from out of nowhere a million tiny things came sweeping straight into my eyes. Even as I went blind, I knew it was a cloud of pepper. And even as I ducked and groped for my gun, I knew it was too damn late. Something hit me a terrific clip on the top of my poor head. My legs went out from under me, and all the colored comets in the heavens played tag around my scrambled brains.

In a dull hazy sort of way, I was a little bit conscious of hands grabbing me, and seeming to hold me off Mother Earth for the briefest of moments. And then something soft was slapped down over my face. The stifling stench of chloroform registered on my exploding brain, and then I went sailing off into a never-never land of complete silence and darkness.

I was not conscious of the return

journey from that never-never land. To be truthful, I really wasn't conscious of anything. It was all just a swimming blur of this and that. I seemed to be going someplace; moving rather smoothly but without any great amount of speed. There were noises, too, inside my head, and all around the outside. For one brief, lucid moment I distinctly heard a boat whistle, and the rasping blare of car horns. And then the thick muggy curtain closed down again with a rumbling, mumbling sound.

I wanted very much to open my eyes and change a faint spinning glow to clear shapes and outlines. But there seemed to be a ten-pound weight wired to my lids, and I could do nothing at all about them. In fact, I could do nothing at all about any of the muscles in my body.

Time passed, of course, and forward movement continued while I sat there in the middle of nothing, not knowing a thing, and not caring a terrible lot, either. Fortunately, though, my bouncing-back qualities are as good as the next man's, and so little by little I began to get things a little straighter. But I still didn't have an eye I could open, or a muscle I could move.

Anyway, I finally knew that I was in the front seat of a car, and that somebody on my left was driving at a steady road-covering pace. I also could tell I was on a well-traveled road. Other cars passed us going both ways. I felt sure, too, that I was near water. I heard boat whistles, or maybe they were train whistles. I couldn't smell the water. I could only smell the sickening stench of chloroform that seemed to hang in a cloud right under my nose.

If only I could move! Just my hand. Reach out with my left and grab whoever was driving the car. Just that little bit would tell me a lot, and I wanted to know a lot. But the combination of that bang on the head, and the chloroform, was still much too much for me. I couldn't move even a fingertip.

More time passed, but I didn't improve any. I even began to slip back a little. The tiny corner of my brain that was trying desperately to function with a fair amount of clarity seemed to break off and become all mangled up by the whizzing stars and comets. And then, just when it seemed that nothing in the world could save me from sinking under again for good, the person driving the car turned it sharply to the left and put on the brakes. My whole body jerked, but I didn't have anything to do with jerking it.

An instant later, I could tell that the driver was reaching across in front of me and opening the door on my side. I knew it, and that's all. But I was unable to catch what followed. Fingers fumbled at my neck. In the middle of a sudden blaze of white light, I thought that my necktie was being pulled tighter. I was having the Lord's own trouble to breathe. And then . . . and perhaps it's true that those who are about to die see all and understand all for one fleeting split second . . . I knew that it was not my tie being pulled tighter and tighter. It was a thin, strong wire. And it was digging deeper and deeper into the flesh of my neck.

Exactly what I did then, or how I did it, I'll never know. When your head is exploding with all the sounds possible in the world, you're unable to retain things for future consideration. All that I can say is, while my head exploded and a sheet of seething flame wrapped itself about my chest, I was falling over sideways. To my right, and down. From upwards and behind me I heard a yell, but it was so garbled and muffled by the explosions in my head that I couldn't tell whether it was from joy or from rage.

I was simply falling, straight down. Then white pain in one shoulder told me that I had hit something hard. I seemed to bounce, and hang motionless in the middle of nothing. And then I started falling, down, and down, and down. Maybe my arms were flung out, and maybe my feet were kicking at nothing. I don't know. But without warning, I hit water. It closed over me with a terrific roar of sound. And a million unseen hands grabbed me and dragged me deeper and deeper.

The band of seething flame wrapped about my chest became tighter and tighter and seemed to be forcing all of my insides up into my throat. But there they were forced to stop because my brains were pushing their way down from above. Air! That was what I wanted. But there wasn't any air. There was nothing but cold dark water that engulfed me and sucked me down toward the center of the earth. But the engulfing water had done one thing. It had returned the power to move my muscles.

As I went sinking, I tore at my neck with both hands; with all my ten fingers. But I could not even wedge a fingertip under that thin wire. It seemed sunk an inch in my neck all the way around. Somehow — and that I will never know either — I managed to get my hands around to the back of my neck and find the two ends of the wire that had been crimped over. I went at them like crazy; the frantic, berserk efforts of a man well into the middle of the throes of death. The sharp ends dug into my fingertips and tore the flesh, but I did not feel the pain. I was well beyond the point where one can distinguish a new pain from the hundreds already consuming the body.

Suddenly the fire circling my throat went away. Convulsively I sucked in air.

Only it wasn't air, it was water. But it did put out the flames in my chest, although it touched off two times the thunder that had been roaring in my head. But I didn't mind the thunder because at that instant I broke surface. My face came up out of the water and there was air. Choking, gasping, and coughing up the soles of my shoes, I fought for that air. I wanted buckets of it, but I seemed able only to get a drop at a time.

I forced myself to relax as much as I could, and float on my back. I couldn't see anything because my eyeballs felt turned backwards in their sockets, and I was simply looking at the fireworks still raging in my brain. But the drops added up, and presently I was able to take a fair amount of air into my burning lungs and gain the benefits from it. And a short time later I was able to roll over, and tread water, and begin to see things.

It took time, though, to see things clearly and make any sense out of them. But I finally did. I saw that I was about twenty yards out and sixty yards down from the end of the Seventy-Second

Street pier. There was nothing on the pier. No automobile that had carried me to the edge. I knew then that my shoulder had hit the string-piece at the end, and that I had bounced off it and down into the water. That there was neither car nor human being on the pier indicated that my would-be killer had decided that the water would finish me, and had driven away.

I was very happy that that was not so. I was so happy that I blew my top a little and cried and laughed hysterically there in the wet Hudson River. But maybe it was just what I needed. When I stopped, I felt pretty good. Full of pain, of course, but I had just about all of my strength back. Anyway, more than enough to swim to shore and drag myself up onto dry land. I sat down and rested for a few minutes. Then I got slowly to my feet, squeezed what water I could from my clothes, and made my way across the Express High-way, and up onto Seventy-Second Street where Riverside begins. The third taxi I waved at swung over to a stop and took me aboard.

When I let myself into my apartment, the clock on my desk said twenty minutes after two. Pulling off my soggy clothes, I went straight into the kitchenette to the Scotch bottle and poured myself the stiffest drink a man can take and not fall down boom. I hung onto the sink while the drink hit me in all parts at the same time. Then I went out into the living room and over to the phone. With a finger that didn't hurt as much as the others, I dialed Centre Street Police Headquarters. I finally got Bierman.

'This is Barnes,' I said. 'I'm in my apartment, you know the address. Jump in your prowl car and come up here fast.'

'Come what?' he blew up over the phone. 'Me come there this time of morning? What in hell do you — '

'Save it!' I cut in on him savagely. 'If you want to be in on the final act, come up here *now*. If you don't want to, then go to hell!'

I broke the connection with a bang and headed for the shower saying words I had not even thought of since the war.

22

At eight thirty the next morning, I was standing on the corner of one of the Eighties and Park Avenue. Not exactly standing, though. I mean I was strolling up and down like an early shopper waiting for the stores to open up. However, I was only there to keep my eyes open and see all that there was to see.

At ten minutes after nine, a whole lot of fears and doubts began to churn around inside of me, picking up more and more speed with every revolution. This was the morning. It just had to be. If it turned out no soap, I'd have to figure out another angle and run the fifty-fifty risk of figuring one out too late. And so by the time the minute hand of my watch was pointing at the half hour, I was as jumpy as a new bride, and twice as worried.

Half a dozen times I started to cross the avenue when the cross light was green, but each time I forced myself to go back and do some more looking. It was tough to make myself do that. Worry that I had figured things wrong sent my imagination into a beautiful flat spin. I imagined more cockeyed things there on that corner than I have ever imagined all together in my life. And that, added to the way I felt physically, was hard to take. I promised myself that after another fifteen minutes, I'd take things into my own hands and let the flying chips fall to earth where they might.

Fortunately, that was one problem I didn't have to solve. At twenty-two minutes to ten, the door of the apartment building kitty-cornered across the street from me swung open, and out came Zara Zaralis with a beaming, cheery-faced doorman at her heels. She carried one of those WAC shoulder-strap bags about the size of a small trunk, and she looked quite the cute little thing as she waited while Cheery Face peeped his whistle and waved at passing taxicabs.

For a crazy instant, I was almost tempted to cross over and say a pleasant good morning. But I didn't. Maybe she wouldn't have been happy to see me. After all, the lady had given the Barnes the bum's rush, had she not? So I curbed the desire and hugged the drugstore doorway, and watched her trip lightly into a cab that eventually swerved into the curb empty.

Still hugging the store doorway, I watched it drive up the avenue and turn west at the next street. Life was beginning again for me, but I waited until my watch said quarter to ten. Then I crossed over, walked into her building lobby, flicked a passing salute to the doorman who didn't know me from Adam, and stepped into one of the punch-button elevators.

Being the careful type, I got out at sixteen and walked down two flights of fire-exit stairs to fourteen. In front of Goldilocks' apartment door I stopped, took a deep breath, and then did a retake. I pushed the bell button and waited, with every nerve I've got twanging like an off-key violin string. Nobody opened the door, so I jabbed the bell again. No answer. I pushed the bell button the third time for luck. I got the kind of luck I wanted. Nobody opened the door.

The ring-chain of keys Maurice Cardeur had once owned I had in my hands by then. I selected one I thought would do the trick, but it didn't. Nor the second I selected, either. I forced down rising disappointment, and panic, and selected a third. That was the one. I opened the apartment door easy as pie, stepped in quickly, and softly closed it. Then I stood there two, three minutes not moving a single thing except my eyes.

And I moved them in all directions at the same time. But I didn't see a single thing save a hundred things that drew a picture of Goldilocks in my mind right away. Finally I moved slowly through the foyer and down into the half sunken living room. There was some Scotch on the little coffee table, but I was strong. Also, I was damned uneasy, and I guess you could call it a little scared. I mean, the old familiar feeling was crawling across the back of my neck and down along my backbone to the end of my spine. The feeling that danger was silently picking the spot before letting fly with the haymaker. I sensed that I was not alone in that apartment!

Turning so that my back was to a wall that had neither door nor window with heavy drapes, I eased out my gun and slipped off the safety catch. Doing that made me feel better, but not a hell of a lot. If I wasn't alone in that place, then he or she was unquestionably following my every move. Maybe even smothering a laugh because of the gun in my hand. I suddenly had the insane urge to yell: *Come out, come out, wherever you are, goddammit!*

I choked off the urge, naturally, but I didn't move. I took in every detail of that room and what I could see beyond the three doors that led off it. Every single little detail, and I think all of them are stamped on my memory for the rest of my life. But not one thing that I looked at and studied minutely could I turn into a human being.

Presently, little by little, that old familiar feeling began to go away. But my folks did not raise any crazy children. I played it very, very safe all the way around, and all over. All over that flossy apartment. With both myself and my gun ready for anything, I toured Goldilocks' apartment like nobody's business, but nobody jumped me, or shot at me, or even said, 'Boo!'

When it was all over, and I was back in the living room, I knew a whole lot more than when I had started. I knew things like how many gowns Zara had, and that she was stocked up enough to go into the lingerie business any time she wanted, and even set up a perfume and cosmetics shop as a sideline. But about things that mattered, nothing at all at the moment.

Back in the living room I holstered my gun, dropped myself comfortably onto the sofa, and gave myself up to waiting. Just how long I wasn't sure, but I had a feeling that it wouldn't be too long. Could be I was wrong, though. Very wrong about a number of things, and the net result would add up to one of the messiest jams the Barnes had ever found himself in the middle of.

All my little nerves started softly

jingling-jangling some more, and I was eying the Scotch bottle and wondering if a short nip would soothe them when the phone bell let go in the bedroom.

Like in the movies and storybooks, I sat like a man of stone trying to hold my breath but breathing heavily just the same. The damn thing rang again, and I was half up on my feet before I could stop myself. Like a million other people, I just can't resist not answering a ringing telephone. Good news or bad, I've just got to know.

But this was once when I didn't. I stayed put, and after it had rasped my nerves for the sixth time, the phone shut up and stayed that way. And I reached for the Scotch to pour myself one that I really needed badly. Unfortunately, though, that two fingers of straight Scotch never reached my lips!

It was halfway there when I heard, or sensed, the swift, sudden, desperate movement. It was like a couple of dozen times in Burma, and China, and in the Philippines. The whisper of death on its way fast. You hear it, or you just sense it. It doesn't matter which. If you've been trained for that sort of thing — or better still, met up with it in actual experience a few times — you do the absolutely correct thing instinctively. Your brain giving orders to your muscles has nothing to do with it. It's all done and finished before you've even begun to think.

So, of course, I didn't twist my head around for a flash look in back of me. Or even start up onto my feet. On the contrary, I threw myself over sidewise and twisted the middle part of me over and down, so that I landed on my hands and knees on the floor. By then he had brought down the barrel of his gun. He couldn't stop in time. Neither the gun, nor his forward movement. The gun smacked the sofa cushion halfway down. The forward movement banged him against the back of the sofa. As he sort of cartwheeled, I zoomed up. I locked both hands around his gun wrist, pivoted, and twisted my hands at the same time.

The gun fell from his fingers, and his body was draped over my hunched back for about two split seconds. Then, using arm leverage, *his* arm, I hurled him in a flying arc that ended up with him flat on his back on the floor.

Gordon Parrish was tough, though. Considerably tougher than I would have believed. The average man would have had barely a drop of air left in his lungs, and most certainly he would have had a broken wrist. But he had air, and he still had two arms to use. He came up like a rubber ball and charged head first. Yes, by then I could have had my gun out, or grabbed up his, and done my stuff. But I didn't want it that way. This character I wanted to take with my bare hands. Stage stuff? Maybe. But bear in mind that it was *my* head that had been lumped plenty two nights before.

Anyway, I let him charge. A little bit. Then I moved in between his outflung hands and let him have one. I cracked my first to the front of his neck, to the Adam's apple. And practically at the same time, I brought my left down on the back of his neck. Right at the hairline, to be exact. Sure, his charging body hurtled full force against me, and I am not constructed along immovable brick-wall lines. I went flying over backwards, but the sofa was there, so I actually sat down hard. And with quite a bit of my wind gone. But there was no sofa for Parrish. There was only the floor. He hit it flat on his face, half rolled over and clawed frantically at his neck. His face was a pretty purple, and his eyes were bugging out because he couldn't get air down through his fist-squashed windpipe.

He would be able to in time, though, so I proceeded to indicate that he should cease all efforts to battle. I got a handful of his jacket and shirt with my left hand, hoisted him up a foot or so off the floor, and then smashed his potato-shaped nose with my right, letting go my hold as I did so. I had long ago counted six lumps on my head, so I went through that routine six times. And each time I hit him in a different place. Believe me, he was twice as homely when the seventh time I hoisted him all the way up and flung him back onto the sofa. Then I backed up to a chair and sat down. With regret, I noticed that the coffee table only had two good legs, and that a bottle of perfectly good Scotch was making a two-inch-thick scatter rug soaking wet.

Still and all, I didn't feel too sorry. I even felt good, to tell the truth. It was nice to know that I was still in pretty good form, and that civilian life had not as yet dulled any of the edges, or thrown my timing out of whack. Yes, I felt very good indeed as I watched him sit head thrown back, his two hands stroking his throat, and his blood-smeared puffed lips grabbing for air. His gun was on the floor at his feet, but I made no move to pick it up and put it out of harm's way. Instead I took out my own gun, and held it lightly in my hand. Maybe I was simply trying to bait him into going for his gun, I don't know. Anyway, when he finally brought his head down, and glared at me out of the one eye that was still open, he didn't move any other part of him. I just grinned.

'How did you get in, Parrish?' I finally asked him. 'And where were you hiding? I thought I'd really gone over this place.'

Truthfully, I wasn't terribly interested

in those answers. They were just by way of starting a conversation. Actually, he was the last person in the world I had expected to see that morning. I thought I had taken care of one Gordon Parrish. Obviously, *very* obviously, I hadn't.

'I should have shot you, Barnes!'

Because of his fist-damaged throat, and a few other clouts, it was hard for him to talk. His words sounded like the bricks of a lightning-struck chimney sliding down an asphalt-shingled roof.

'You should have done a lot of things,' I told him flatly. I gave him a couple of moments to make out of that whatever he wanted to. 'A whole lot of things,' I then said. 'One of the big ones being to take a hint when you were given one yesterday at the Biltmore. How did you get in here?'

He glared at me with his good eye, sneered at me with his lips, and said nothing. Well, if he wanted to play that way, it was perfectly all right with me. I came out of my chair fast, took the two necessary steps and raked the left side of his face from the temple to the jaw point with the muzzle of my gun. He howled with pain as the little drops of blood oozed through.

'How did you get in?' I repeated, and moved back to my chair.

'The same way you did,' he groaned, and put a hand to his face. 'It was nothing.'

'Where'd you come from just now?' I wanted to know.

He moved his head a little to indicate a big padded chair in the corner. I glanced that way, and felt very silly. It looked like the last thing in the whole place someone would hide behind. I guess that's why I had completely overlooked it. However, it didn't matter now. I fixed my gaze on Parrish again, and gave him a slow smile.

'Now the sixty-four-dollar question,' I said. 'Just what were you doing, or did you hope to do, in here?'

I thought I knew, or at least could make a damn close guess. I wanted to hear it from his lips, though. However, I didn't. I didn't because at that exact instant, I heard a key being fitted into the apartment front door lock. Parrish heard it, too. He stiffened up a little. By then, though, I was moving fast.

I went over to him and brought my gun barrel down across his head. He folded, and rolled off the sofa onto the floor. I gave him a shove with my foot to a position where he wouldn't be seen at once from the foyer. Then, holstering my gun, I walked quickly to the foyer, along the wall against which the door would open. I reached it just in time to slide out of sight as the door opened. The balloon was at long last going up — I hoped!

23

Goldilocks came in in a hurry, slammed the door shut and went three or four steps along the foyer. Then she stopped dead like a little wild animal suddenly sensing danger. I was in back of her, of course, and saw her stiffen rigid. She had spotted the busted coffee table, and the liquor-soaked scatter rug, and maybe Parrish's feet sticking out from behind the sofa. She sucked in air loudly, clutched the strap of her WAC bag with her left hand, and started to put her right in her coat pocket.

'Hello, Zara,' I said pleasantly.

For the briefest part of an instant, she didn't move. Then she whirled in a flash, diving her hand into her coat pocket and out with a little French derringer pistol. But I was right on top of her then. I had her wrist, and was twisting hard. She dropped the gun and came at my face with the clawing fingers of her other hand. I jerked my head to the side and hit her. I hit her hard and dumped her in a little heap on the floor. No, not gentlemanly, and certainly not gallant. But I have certain rules about women. Whenever one of them tries to shoot me, I always hit her if I can.

I reached down and picked up the little derringer and dropped it in my jacket pocket. Then I hoisted her up onto her feet. She was groggy but not completely out. Finally I picked up her WAC bag that had slid off her shoulder. It felt like she had filled it full of BB shot. And I stood there gently but firmly holding her right arm while she shook most of the cobwebs away. She finally looked up at me out of blazing eyes, and spat out a string of stuff that made me feel sure she was originally from Greece, because the words she spat out were all so much Greek to me. I shook my head down at her.

'No I'm not, Goldilocks,' I said, and grinned. 'But I must've given you a shock after last night, eh?'

She tried to wrench her arm free, and gave it up. She stood quiet as a mouse looking up at me with the damnedest expression. I thought that any instant the come-hither smile was going to show. But it didn't.

'You are mad!' she said through tight teeth. 'What is the meaning of this thing? You will tell me now, this moment!'

'I'll tell you, Goldie,' I said, 'but not right now. I'm expecting . . .'

I didn't finish because what I was expecting came about. The apartment door bell sounded sharply, and knuckles banged hard on the other side. I turned Goldilocks around and walked her back the few steps to the door. I pulled it open, and there stood Lieutenant Frank Bierman. Right behind him was the ever-present Sergeant Goff. Maybe there were other cops in the hallway, but I didn't stick my head out to look. I smiled at Bierman and jerked my head.

'Come in, Lieutenant, and you too, Sergeant,' I said. 'The party's just about to begin.'

Bierman looked at me hard, and at Zara a little bit harder. Then he looked past both of us, and his eyes narrowed a little.

'This way, gentlemen,' I said.

As I said it, I turned Zara around and, still holding her arm, led the way into the living room. When Goldilocks spotted who was on the floor behind the sofa, she let out a funny little hissing sound. I paid no attention, though. I seated her in a chair all for her, let go of her arm, and stepped back to smile again at Bierman and Sergeant Goff. It was my moment, and I was loving it.

'Sorry I can't offer you a drink, gentlemen,' I said. 'The rug seems to have taken it all.'

'All right with the horsing around, Barnes!' Bierman snapped. 'I've done my part, what I promised you last night. I followed her to the bank and back here. She didn't go anyplace else. All right, now I'm listening. I want all of it. I want every damn bit of what you wouldn't tell me last night. Take your time, because no one's going anyplace yet.'

The echo to Bierman's voice was a long drawn-out groan from Gordon Parrish on the floor. He pushed up slowly on his hands and knees, and then just his knees.

His eyes blinked stupidly at us, and then rapidly as faces became recognizable. Finally his eyes popped, and his lips worked up and down, but he seemed unable to get any words out from between them. I reached down and hooked a hand under his shoulder and hoisted him up onto the sofa. He fell back on it like a sack of wet meal, his lips still working like a carp's out of water.

'Go ahead and begin, Barnes!' Bierman barked. 'And be damn sure you begin at the beginning! Who the devil is he?'

'The name's Gordon Parrish,' I told him. 'And as he's just joined the party, I might as well begin with him.'

'Then *do* it!' Bierman growled when I didn't keep right on talking.

I nodded and looked at Parrish for a moment. 'Stop me if and where I go wrong,' I told him. And then to Bierman, 'Parrish was the client I met right after you'd thrown me out of my office. He wanted to hire me to find Maurice Cardeur, who'd been missing ever since he walked out of the Rankins' brawl. He was afraid something had happened to

Cardeur as a result of that near scrap, and he didn't dare go to the police. He wanted to get in touch with Cardeur for reasons you'll learn as we go along with this thing. Anyway, I took the job, but didn't tell him that I knew DeFoe was dead. He found that out later from the newspapers, and when he thought back over things I'd said, he got scared. In other words, just how much did I know about a lot of things? So he got another one of them, one Franz Eurlich, to tail me. He was the lad I thought was your man.'

I paused and gave Bierman a chance to speak, but he just nodded for me to go on.

'Eurlich, of course, reported to Parrish that I'd gone to see Goldilocks, Miss Zara Zaralis,' I said. 'That added to his frightened confusion. By the way, Parrish, was that taxicab act your idea, or did Eurlich suggest it? He seems the type.'

Parrish acted as though he hadn't heard, and I didn't mind. I knew he'd howl if I really went off the track.

'Parrish didn't like that at all,' I said

again. 'He decided to really find out what I knew. Which, by the way, was damn little at that point. Anyway, I fell for the old taxi trick, and got my head caved in. I woke up in that room I told you about. The guy who asked the questions was Eurlich. Parrish was there, but he didn't dare ask them because he was afraid I'd recognize his voice. Well, I wasn't able to give the answers wanted because I didn't know them. DeFoe hadn't told me a damn thing. But I made a crack that caused Parrish to believe I knew who'd finished DeFoe. He thought I meant him. He lost his head. His hired thugs beat me up, stripped me of everything, and dumped me into the East River. That turned out bad for him, because I didn't die. Instead, I woke up in a place that is no place for a chap of my clean habits.'

I paused, but Bierman didn't think that funny at all. I made a little skip-it gesture, and continued.

'Yesterday when I phoned Parrish and made a date to see him, he sounded like he was close to fainting. Naturally, he had to see me. He wanted it at his place, with

Eurlich there in case I'd added up a couple of things and wanted to do something about it. He also wanted the answer to Cardeur's sudden disappearance. When I told him Cardeur was dead, that knocked the pins out from under him. All he wanted then was to pay me off and get rid of me. He was beginning to add up this and that himself. Eurlich, the dope, pulled a nutty act to convince me that he and Parrish had had nothing to do with either murder. He called me a liar and started to muss me up. I had to make it the other way around. I collected the thousand Parrish owed me for finding Cardeur dead or alive, and left. Which reminds me.'

I suddenly stepped over to Parrish and turned back the front of his jacket, and took out his wallet from the inside pocket. There was quite a bit of Uncle Sam green inside. I took fifteen hundred dollars of it, put it in my pocket, and dropped the wallet in his lap. All the time he didn't move a muscle. He was finally getting some sense into that head of his!

'The fifteen hundred you took from

me, Parrish,' I said quietly. 'What part of it you had to pay those hired thugs is your loss.'

I expected Bierman to open up then, but he fooled me. He simply narrowed his eyes a little and focused them more intently upon me.

'When I left Parrish, he was more worried than before,' I said. 'He tried to get in touch with me through Paula. She told him I'd be at the Biltmore around five. He invited her there for a drink, and tried to pump her, figuring I'd told her a thing or two. When I showed up, he faked it that he wanted to apologize for Eurlich's nutty stunt. By then, Parrish wasn't in my thoughts anymore. I knew for sure that he wasn't the one I was after. I gave him a broad hint to curl up and go to sleep some-place until a later date. He didn't take the hint. He'd added things up and got an answer — Zara Zaralis. He came here this morning, probably to poke around, and no doubt choke a few things out of her when she returned. I came in instead. So his first task was to take care of me. Well, I just don't like people like Parrish to take care of me. We were just getting chatty when Zara put her key in the door. I had to pop Parrish because I couldn't be bothered watching two people at the same time. And that, I guess, is that regarding Parrish. Any corrections, or additions?'

The last I fired at Parrish. He looked at me like a man watching the whole world falling away from him. Then he sighed heavily, and let his chin sag down on his chest. I looked at Bierman, and grinned. He was still looking at me, but not grinning.

'Very interesting!' he said dryly. 'All those words and gestures to tell me he didn't kill DeFoe or Cardeur.'

'No, he didn't,' I admitted. 'But he tried to kill *me*!'

Bierman grunted and made a gesture as though to say, what the hell did my being alive or dead have to do with DeFoe and Cardeur? 'Who did?' he bit off.

'Who did what?' I asked pleasantly.

'Stop right there, Barnes!' he warned. 'No games today. *Who scragged DeFoe and Cardeur?*'

'It wasn't one person,' I said.

Bierman started and swayed forward on his toes. 'What's that?' he barked.

'Maurice Cardeur killed René DeFoe,' I said. 'At the Rankins' party, it was Cardeur who heard me make a date to meet DeFoe in my office the next morning. He got there first, to hear what DeFoe had to say to me. Cardeur was a very practiced guy with somebody else's door locks. When I didn't show up, the golden opportunity must have presented itself to him. So he scragged DeFoe.'

'Why?' Bierman almost shouted.

'To get something DeFoe had,' I replied.

I could almost see Bierman's wheels turning over as he silently counted ten.

'And what was it that DeFoe had, Barnes, if you don't mind?' he bit off word by word.

'The keys to get into a safety deposit box that DeFoe had under the name of Herbert Varney,' I told him. 'I think he'd already gotten hold of DeFoe's Herbert Varney signature, and could forge it well enough so that there wouldn't be any question at the bank. But he didn't have the two keys. He got those off DeFoe in my office. Right, Goldilocks?'

I half turned as I shot the last at her. The little slick chick smiled at me with seductive love on her lips, and blazing white-heat hate in her eyes.

'I do not know,' she said slowly. 'The talk you make is all insane.'

I shrugged, and looked back at Bierman. He was now regarding me with less held-in-check anger, and more puzzled thoughtfulness.

'So somebody else found out and killed Cardeur?' he asked.

'Somebody already knew,' I said. 'In fact, I think that somebody had planned to kill him just as soon as he'd completed the preliminary dirty work.'

'All right, who?' Bierman asked.

'The lady, here,' I said with a side nod of my head. 'Miss Zara Zaralis.'

Bierman looked at her and frowned. She looked back at him and gave him that old Number Three smile. The kid was but definitely good. The theatre had certainly missed a perfect bet. Or maybe she had been on the stage. I didn't know then, and I still don't.

'Do you deny that?' the trained cop in Bierman demanded.

'But certainly,' she said very calmly. 'I tell *Monsieur* Barnes the same thing in this very room. It is absurd. Maurice Cardeur is my life. I love him. I am his life, also, for he love me like that, too. One does not kill what fills all of one's heart.'

'Not much one doesn't!' I shouted, and then caught myself. 'Listen, Goldilocks, I'll give you the same opportunity I gave Parrish. We'll go over a few things, and you can correct me if and where I go wrong.'

She flashed Bierman that very special smile again, and then leaned back and regarded me with all the suffering patience in the world.

'Very well, if it amuses you,' she said.

'It doesn't!' I barked, stung a little. 'No part of this whole rotten business amuses me a bit. Not any more than it's going to amuse you, sister, when you sit in the electric chair!'

'Just get on with it, Barnes!' Bierman broke it up. 'Go ahead.'

'DeFoe's death, and the reason, may

have been Cardeur's original idea,' I said. 'And he'd already told Zara, his girl-friend, what he planned. But my guess is that it was her idea, and she got him to do the original dirty work. Anyway, after Cardeur had walked out of the Rankins' place a lot of his friends started looking for him. One was a man named Henri Barone, and another an ex-GI by the name of Andrew Parkus. Around noon of the day DeFoe died, they dropped in here to see Zara. They knew she and Cardeur were this way and that way, and hoped she could tell them. She could, but she didn't want to. Maybe she didn't know exactly where Cardeur was, but she had a pretty good idea what he was up to, if he hadn't already completed the job. In short, she knew, too, that DeFoe was meeting me at my office. And she probably had a hunch that . . . '

Goldilocks' thrilling laugh made me stop.

'You are very funny, *Monsieur* Barnes!' she said. 'You think perhaps I use . . . what you call . . . the crystal ball?'

'You didn't have to!' I snapped back. 'Your hunch was good enough. Your first slip, baby. You called my apartment, but you didn't call my office, *listed right under it*. You skipped that and called Paula instead.'

I waited for her to laugh some more, but she didn't. She only smiled, but it was considerably on the frozen side.

'Oh, so she phoned you and you didn't just drop in, like you said, eh?' Bierman's voice batted against my ear. 'Why did she phone you?'

The lieutenant was getting ready to wind up, but I stopped him with a raised hand. 'You're getting it *all* now,' I said quickly. 'Phoning me was her contribution to the mysterious disappearance of Cardeur. To make her two friends feel something could be done to find him. They couldn't go to the police, you see, because they didn't want *any* police attention, considering the business they were in. So — '

'What the devil do you mean, business they were in?' Bierman cut in on me.

'Later,' I brushed it aside. 'So Zara, knowing I was a private dick, got me to run over and take the job of finding Cardeur. Fine. And because Zara's the kind of gal who likes to play with new toys, she decided to confine my hunting Cardeur to her apartment for a few hours or more. But Cardeur phoned her with the news. She made a date to meet him later, and told him to go hide up some place but good. Then she got rid of me. She didn't want me around anymore because she had plans to think up and arrange. I left, and you know what happened to me.'

I stopped again, and looked at her. 'Was the letter to the safety deposit vault guard identifying you as Herbert Varney's messenger already written, and signed Herbert Varney by Cardeur?' I asked. 'Or did you write it that afternoon, and he signed it when you met?'

She was a very cool one with that little bewildered look. 'You tell us so many the things,' she said with a little shrug. 'Can you not tell us that also, no?'

'Sure,' I came right back. 'It was already written, or typed, and signed Herbert Varney by Cardeur. You, Goldilocks, are a woman who always plans for the future. Anyway, you met Cardeur. Being a love-good sap, he didn't suspect a thing. He gave you the safety deposit box keys. And you let him have something very hard on his head. Then you cleaned his pockets, and found the rest of the coil of wire he had used on DeFoe. You tied a wire necktie for him . . . very tight, and dumped him into the Hudson. Off the Seventy-Second Street pier, wasn't it?'

She wouldn't answer. She would only smile; really turning it on when she switched her eyes from me to Bierman.

'Goodbye, sweet Maurice!' I mocked her. 'But you slipped again. The tide wasn't going out, so it didn't take him down to the Narrows where he'd *maybe* be picked up but completely unrecogniz-able. The tide was coming in, and it took Cardeur upstream to Ninety-Sixth Street, where Lieutenant Bierman's boys fished him out. When you found that out from me, you were really in a dither. And when I dropped the name Herbert Varney, you really were stunned. How in hell did I find out about Herbert Varney? That's what you wondered, didn't you? And as you had to say something in front of Barone, and Parkus and me too, you cooked up that one about Parrish being the villain. It stank, baby. Way up to high heaven. So you gave Barone and Parkus the rush because you wanted to work on me. But you couldn't throw any strikes past me, so you threw me out again. This time you really had to do a Garbo and think!'

I gave her a chance to say something. But it was still just the smile, a trifle stiffer. Anyway, the lady didn't want to say anything.

'You came up with the grand idea,' I went on. 'When murder really gets rolling, it's hard to stop. Gerry Barnes had to join René and Maurice. You got Barone to get me to come up to his place. You . . . '

I paused and nodded my grudging praise. 'You were really good,' I said. 'I walked right into it with both eyes open, but you closed them very neatly, and pulled down the blackout curtain. I guess you really must have been a big help in the underground. TNT in a small package. The only thing that went wrong was that I wouldn't die and go away. I either fell, or you pushed me, out of that car on the

Seventy-Second Street pier, before the wire had been twisted enough. Anyway, here I am. And there you are . . . fresh back from the bank. How's it sound, Goldilocks?'

She was wonderful. My God, the dough she could have made playing life on the safe side of the street. She fairly beamed at me, and clapped her hands with enthusiasm.

'Wonderful, superb!' she cried. 'Do you not agree, Lieutenant Bierman? He should write the book. But no! There is but the one very bad mistake!'

'You name it, sister,' I challenged.

'But certainly.' She bobbed her head and continued to beam. 'That, also, I told you in this very room. Maurice was mad with jealousy and came here to punish me. He was a fool. The pepper he throw in my eyes, too. But I know that it is Maurice, even though I cannot see him. I know, you hear? And like I tell you, the lady in the next apartment, she stay with me all the night. So you make the great big mistake about Zara, no?'

'No.' I grinned at her. 'It wasn't Maurice.'

'It was!' she screamed. 'I swear it. A woman, she can tell. It was my Maurice!'

To prove it, she started to cry, and then stopped when I just stood there grinning down at her, and shaking my head. 'It was Maurice!' she managed doggedly.

'Goldilocks,' I told her gravely, 'you sank yourself when you pulled that gag about Maurice coming here and beating you up. You beat yourself up, baby. You wanted the others to think that Cardeur was alive, until he had floated away forever. A few days, or a week, would be swell. You'd be in the clear. But the tide took him the wrong way. *He was found too soon.*' I let her have that with all stops out. And then I let her have the rest. 'It was at eleven thirty that you say Cardeur was here beating you up. But Lieutenant Bierman happens to *know* that he died at nine o'clock! So now what?'

She looked at me, then at Bierman, and then back at me again. 'That could not be so,' she said in a hollow voice. 'It is also not so that I try to kill you last night. I am here all the time, in this place.'

'Look, Goldie, give it up,' I said wearily.

'There's a bit about last night I haven't mentioned yet. When I didn't die, I got very sore at Barone and you. I went back to his place, hoping you two were there. You weren't, but he was. We had a little argument, but I hit the hardest. He decided to save his hide and talk. He talked for a long time, Zara. I'll tell you, though, that he was really stunned to hear about you. The poor fish didn't even suspect. You'd actually sold him on Parrish. When you made him phone me, he didn't even question why. Deep, secret love, that was Barone. He'd always jump through hoops for you, the dope. I had to tie him up good, and lock him in, so he wouldn't change his mind and run away. Lieutenant Bierman will be going up there pretty soon. Maybe he'll take you along, and you can see for yourself I'm not kidding.'

As emphasis for my words Gordon, Parrish groaned and buried his face in his hands. Goldilocks didn't utter a sound. She just turned whiter, and whiter, and whiter. I held out her WAC bag to Bierman. 'She brought you this from the bank,' I said.

He took it, squinting hard at me. Then he pulled the snap flap and lifted it up. When he looked inside, his eyes bugged way out, and he almost dropped the bag. 'God A'mighty!' he gasped hoarsely.

I leaned over for a look, and my eyes bugged out, too. The thing was filled to the brim with diamonds. Hundreds and hundreds of, them, all sizes, cut and uncut.

24

I finally broke the feather-hitting-feather silence. 'Pretty, aren't they?' I murmured.

Bierman jerked his head up, and the old fireball glare was back in his eyes. 'Why the hell didn't you tell me about these?' he rasped out. 'My God, Barnes, she might have — '

'No,' I stopped him. 'She didn't have the chance to go to the bank yesterday. Me and too many of her friends popping in and out. I checked last night, anyway. She didn't leave here during the hours the bank was open. And when she went for me last night, I was sure it'd be first thing this morning. So I got you to promise to tail her, and grab her in case she didn't come back here. You see, it'd take time and a court order, and all kinds of red tape, for us to have that box opened. Easier for her to do it and bring it all back here. Right?'

'What the hell was DeFoe doing with

all these?' Bierman asked sharply. 'My God, they must be worth millions.'

'Several millions is my guess,' I said. 'Technically, DeFoe was the safekeeper. The head man of the bunch. He — '

'What bunch?' Bierman cut in.

'Just shut up and listen,' I said. 'Barone told it all to me in great detail, but I'll cut it down and give you just a rough idea for now. When the Nazis went thundering across Europe, they looted every country high and dry. One of their specialties was diamonds. They raided Antwerp, Amsterdam, Paris, lots of places. But all of the stones didn't quite get back to Germany. Individual Nazi greed. The underground boys knew about that. They had those lads pegged. And when the Nazis went thundering back across Europe a damn sight faster, certain members of the underground moved in quick. They went picking up small hidden caches of diamonds like you'd pick up fallen apples. Oh, only a few did it, but those who did had a good thing for themselves.'

I paused for breath, and Bierman nodded slowly. 'René DeFoe was the leader of an underground unit that included Cardeur, Parrish, Zara, Barone, Eurlich, and some others. To go sell their loot direct to merchants in Antwerp, and elsewhere, would be to ask for a rope around their necks. So they figured out a plan. DeFoe and Barone had connections here in the States. They could sell their loot here a little at a time, and it'd eventually find its way to the European markets. But how to get the diamonds from Europe here? They worked out a very neat smuggling stunt. Each of them took a few, cleverly hidden, and came here for a visit. Believe it or not, the ones I've named to you have made four trips since V-Day. DeFoe came here, though, and stayed. The diamonds were delivered to him, and he worked the deals that brought the cash. DeFoe was smart. He loved them all dearly, but he didn't trust one of them. So he put all the unsold diamonds in a safety deposit box under a name that only he knew. That way — '

'Cardeur knew!' Bierman broke in.

I started to nod, but checked myself, and looked at Zara. 'How did Cardeur find out?' I asked.

'He did not trust René,' she said quietly. 'He search René's rooms, and find a letter to Herbert Varney from the bank. He do that to protect us. We are all beginning to distrust René a little. He is acting strange. We are worried.'

I tossed a glance about that flossy apartment, and looked back at her again. 'Yes, it must have worried you a lot,' I grunted, and turned to Bierman. 'Well, Cardeur found out. He told Zara, and the murder idea was born. Nobody will ever know, but I think DeFoe figured something was in the wind. I mean, that one of his bunch really had definite ideas. So he wanted to hire me to snoop around and find out what I could. Anyway, there are your stones, and I'll leave it to you and the FBI, and all the others, to decide what to do with the money left in DeFoe's checking account. Not to mention what to do about all those sparkling beauties, *and* the people concerned.'

'That damn little black book!' Bierman said, as though he hated like the devil to say it. 'Those addresses — '

'Check,' I cut in. 'By the way, that ex-GI, Andy Parkus, works for one of them. I found that out by simply calling all six of the ones in New York and asking if he worked there. The sixth call got me the information that he did. Just how deep he is in the thing, you can find out for yourself.'

Bierman nodded slowly, and I turned to Zara Zaralis. Her face was not so white now. It had turned a sort of sickish yellow. 'What parts did I have wrong?' I asked quietly.

She looked at me with a little smile, and shrugged. 'Does it make the matter?' she said.

'No, I guess not. One thing, though. Was it your idea, or Cardeur's?'

She didn't reply at once. She just brightened her smile a little, and damned if I didn't want to shiver. It gave me the creeps.

'It was all mine, the idea,' she said, still holding that screwy bright smile. 'I tell Maurice to search the rooms. I say to him I am sure he will find something. He does and he tells me. But we have not the keys.

I tell Maurice that it is better for me, a lady, to go to the bank with the letter of identification from Herbert Varney. Men, they do things for someone who is pretty. She makes their brains work bad. Maurice agrees that is best. I am sorry for Maurice, but I am tired. I am bored. I suffer too much in the war. I decide Zara will take all and go far, far, away where no one can find me. I know a way, too, what to do with the diamonds for money. But it is not to be the thing I plan.'

All the time she was talking, I wanted to scream at her to shut up. That damn smile was driving me nuts. You see, I knew, or thought I knew. But I couldn't do a thing. I would be too late; much too late. I could only stand there staring at her, sort of half hypnotized.

'I tell you the something else,' she spoke again. 'I tell you I think I do not like to sit in your American electric chair, no!'

And then she did it! Her tongue moved against one cheek, and then she bit down hard as though cracking a nut with her teeth. And she swallowed instantly. I swear a wisp of smoke passed her lips, but of course that isn't true. But her lips changed from red to purple-black, and she toppled off the chair and down onto the floor.

'What the hell?' Bierman yelled. He started to leap over, but I grabbed his arm.

'No use, Bierman,' I said. 'Himmler pulled the same stunt on the British, and they couldn't do a thing to save him for the rope. She's probably had it around since her underground days when the Gestapo boys were on the prowl. She's . . . Oh hell, man, isn't it better this way?'

★   ★   ★

A half hour or so later, Bierman was standing with me on the sidewalk out front while I tried to catch a cruising taxicab.

'Well, you broke just about all the rules again, Barnes,' he growled. 'But you broke the case, too, so maybe the commissioner won't scream very loud for your license. One thing, though, I still don't get. How did you know that the motive was diamonds, and that they were dealing in them?'

'Hunches, and a good break,' I replied. 'They were all from the other side of the pond. And it was plain none of them wanted anything to do with cops. I got to thinking, and called a couple of friends of mine in Washington and asked if the FBI or the Treasury Department boys were working on any particular thing that had a European angle. They wouldn't tell me, and promised to let me know even less. But one of them sent me a wire. Here, take a look.'

As I pulled the telegram from my pocket and gave it to Bierman, an empty taxi swerved into the curb. I nodded to the driver that he was hired and looked at Bierman. He was staring at me, half bewildered, and half getting sore again fast.

'Before asking Paula, what would you do first?' he spoke the words of the telegram aloud. 'Now, just what in hell did that mean to you, I'd like to know.'

'Nothing at first.' I grinned at him. 'Not until I was about ready to throw myself out the window. Then I got it. I'd buy an engagement ring, of course. Diamonds! Get it?'

'Well, I'll be a . . . ' Bierman gulped and choked.

'Both of us,' I laughed, and pulled open the cab door. 'But speaking of Paula, I promised to buy her the town tonight. How about doing the town with us, Lieutenant? Then I won't have to answer *all* the questions.'

He gravely handed me back the telegram, and kept his hand out as though to ward me off. 'No thank you!' he said with head-shaking emphasis. 'A riot, a strike picket-line battle, or even a fair-sized earthquake, I could take. But doing this town with you and Miss Grant? *That* I couldn't!'

'Why, you great big sissy!' I jeered, and climbed into the cab.

We do hope that you have enjoyed reading this large print book.

Did you know that all of our titles are available for purchase?

We publish a wide range of high quality large print books including:
Romances, Mysteries, Classics
General Fiction
Non Fiction and Westerns

Special interest titles available in large print are:
The Little Oxford Dictionary
Music Book, Song Book
Hymn Book, Service Book

Also available from us courtesy of Oxford University Press:
Young Readers' Dictionary
(large print edition)
Young Readers' Thesaurus
(large print edition)

For further information or a free brochure, please contact us at:
Ulverscroft Large Print Books Ltd.,
The Green, Bradgate Road, Anstey,
Leicester, LE7 7FU, England.
Tel: (00 44) **0116 236 4325**
Fax: (00 44) **0116 234 0205**

Other titles in the
Linford Mystery Library:

YOU CAN'T CATCH ME

Lawrence Lariar

Somewhat against his better judgment, Mike Wells accepts a lucrative assignment from bigtime gangster Rico Bruck. It seems a simple enough job: to board a train and shadow a man on his journey to New York, and then to telephone his whereabouts to Bruck. Mike takes with him the beautiful Toni Kaye, who tells him she wants to escape Bruck's employment and make a career as a singer. But when they arrive at their destination, their target is found murdered . . .